Ernst von Wildenbruch

Harold

Tragedy in five acts

Ernst von Wildenbruch

Harold
Tragedy in five acts

ISBN/EAN: 9783337105556

Printed in Europe, USA, Canada, Australia, Japan

Cover: Foto ©Andreas Hilbeck / pixelio.de

More available books at **www.hansebooks.com**

HAROLD.

TRAGEDY IN FIVE ACTS

BY

ERNST VON WILDENBRUCH.

———

TRANSLATED

BY

MARIE VON ZGLINITZKA.

———

HANOVER 1884.

PUBLISHED BY CARL SCHÜSSLER.

The author reserves to himself and his heirs and successors the entire right of the translation and performance of the following drama.

Printed by Carl Schüssler — Hanover.

Dramatis-Personae.

Edward, King of England.
Gytha, Widow of Earl Godwin.
Harold, Duke of East Anglia, ⎫ her Sons.
Wulfnoth, ⎭
William, named the Conqueror, Duke of Normandy.
Adéle, his daughter.
Earl Morcar, ⎫ Anglo-saxon Nobles, Cousins of Earl Godwin.
Earl Edwin, ⎭
Count Eustace of Boulogne, ⎫
The Seneschal, ⎮
Odo, ⎬ Norman Barons.
Randulf, ⎮
Montgomery, ⎭
Robert of Jumièges, Archbishop of Canterbury.
Stigand, Bishop of Winchester.
The Abbot of Hyde Cloister.
Wilfried, an Anglo-saxon Deacon.
Ordgar, ⎫
Edric, ⎬ Citizens of Dover.
Baldwulf, ⎭
Eleanor, ⎫ Ladies in waiting to Adéle.
Alice, ⎭
An Anglo-saxon ⎫ Heralds.
A Norman ⎭

Citizens. Knights. Retainers.

Time: Before and during the Conquest of England by the
Normans.

Place: Act I.: Dover. Act II.: Rouen and London. Act III.:
Rouen. Act IV.: London. Act V.: Rouen and near Hastings.

Errata — see last page.

Act 1.

(Scene: A spacious Hall in Godwin's castle at Dover. Large windows to the back. Doors R. and L. At the back of the stage a raised dais, steps leading up to it: an arm chair is placed upon it as a throne — seats toward the front of the stage-the walls are hung with armoury.)

Gytha dressed in mourning robes is seated in the foreground.
Bishop Stigand stands before her.

Stigand.

It grieves me noble lady still to see
Upon thy brow the cloud of gloomy sorrow
That ever rests there since Earl Godwin's death.

Gytha.

Still, dost thou say? what wretched word of comfort!
It sounds but strangely from Earl Godwin's friend.

Stigand.'

Because his friend, because my bleeding heart
Each hour recals to me thy bitter loss,
Have I through grief the privilege attained
To pray thee put a curb upon thy sadness.

Gytha (giving him her hand).

Good Bishop Stigand last and truest friend,
How can I chide thee? Nay but say thyself,
Can any thing more bitter poison woe,
And change the aspect of a sacred grief,
More swiftly into mask of angry hate.

1

Than when t'is shown us that the dying hour
Of him with whom our own life passed away,
Was unto others but the longed for signal
Of freedom gained?

Stigand.

To whom then lady?

Gytha.

     Whom?
And thou can'st ask who know'st this realm so well?
Hast known it longer twice ten years than I,
And know'st the ruler of this realm.

Stigand.

    King Edward?

Gytha.

Yes, yes, that king I mean! That very Edward!

Stigand.

And were the tone with which his name thou namest
But a sharp sword with which to pierce his breast,
He'd live no longer.

Gytha.

     Were it but a sword!
Were I a man I would have more than words!

Stigand.

Countess, he is a king.

Gytha.

     By whom then made one?
Who shed his blood for him in hundred battles,
Who checked rebellion's boldly threatening hand
Upraised against him?

2

Stigand.
Well I know.

Gytha.
Earl Godwin!
O every breath of life that he doth draw
Should be a breath of thanks unto my lord.

Stigand.
T'is that I fear me robs thee of his grace,
T'is said that gratitude is hard to bear.

Gytha.
Only for those who are of shallow mind;
The Weakling!

Stigand.
All too loudly speaks thine anger:
Edward is meek but hath a kindly nature.

Gytha.
A kindly nature! Pitiable praise
If it be all that we can give a king.

(Enter **Wulfnoth** led by an attendant from R. [he wears mourning] goes up to
his mother and embraces her.)

Stigand.
See, see, the ancient stem hath left fair blossoms!
(seating himself and drawing the child toward him)
Precious inheritance of him we honoured,
God guard thee well from frost thou sapling green!
(to Gytha)
Where stays thy eldest born the young Duke Harold?

Wulfnoth.
To London gone, to buy for me a sword.

Stigand (taking the child onhis knee).
Thou need'st a sword already little man?

Wulfnoth.
Yes soon I shall be big and then we'll fight,
Harold and I together 'gainst the Normans.

Stigand.
(presses the child passionately to his breast.)
Godwin, thy blood flows in thy children's veins!
I shall not live to see the time my child,
When thou to manhood's years shalt have attained
May'st thou, thou bright young spark-emitting steel
Thyself become a sword for our loved country!

Gytha.
Go now and play my Wulfnoth.
(Stigand places the boy upon the ground) Wulfnoth and attendant exeunt R.)
Hath this child
So moved thee?

Stigand.
Countess I would pray thee tell me
What thoughts thy son, Duke Harold entertains
On present matters of our land?

Gytha.
Ah Bishop,
He is alas, to me almost a stranger,
Scarce have I seen him since my husband's death,
For ceaseless travel draws him ever from me,
Now to the sea — to London — to his lands.

Stigand (looking from window).
See Lady, yonder nobles of our realm
Decked out in robes of latest frankish fashion;
How in despising thus their people's customs,
Their feeling toward their country thy betray.

4

—◄ ACT 1. ►—

(Enter an **Attendant** (announces)).

The noble Earls Lords Edwin and Morcar.

Gytha (aside).

I wonld it were some other.
          (aloud) They are welcome.
          (Attendant opens door L.)

(Enter **Edwin, Morcar** from L. They are gaudily dressed in norman fashion).

Edwin (bending his head).

God greet thee noble cousin.

Morcar.
          Cousin, greeting!

Gytha.

My Lords I bid ye welcome.

Edwin.
          Still in mourning?
Art thou aware the king comes here to day?

Gytha.

The king? To-day? Till now I knew it not:
T'was not announced to me.

Morcar.
          That well may be;
The king needs not to question of his vassals
When t'is their gracious pleasure to receive him.
          (Gytha and Stigand exchange glances.)

Edwin.

Wilt thou receive him in this mourning garb?

5

Gytha.

Yes, if Earl Edwin knows not to advise me
Of dress more suited to Earl Godwin's Widow.

Edwin.

By God in heaven, we know that Godwin died,
But t'was a year ago.

Stigand.

                              My noble Sir
That may be long for this our country's weal
Yet a short space to mourn an honoured husband.

Edwin (to Stigand).

There have been, still are many such as he.

Stigand.

In truth I would that there were many like him.

Morcar.

Bishop, I ask thy pardon for the question:
Is it thy purpose to await the king?

Stigand.

With Countess Gytha's gracious leave — it is.

Morcar.

I am aware thou art my cousin's guest,
But yet permit as eldest of our house
That I should tell thee what thou know'st right well,
The king hath little pleasure in thy presence.

Stigand.

And wherefore not? —

Morcar.

Thou know'st the reason, Bishop:
Thou art the leader of the ill-affected,
Thou much dost hate our Lord of Canterbury
Robert Jumièges, because he is a Norman,
And faintest sparks of deeply hidden rage
Scattered amidst our people thousandfold,
Are fanned by trust in thee into a flame.

Stigand.

And thou belong'st not to this people?

Morcar.

No!
Our house doth nothing know of discontent.

Harold (enters unperceived from L. and remains standing. He wears mourning and his long fair hair falls in waving curls over his shoulders in contrast to the closely cut locks of Edwin and Morcar).

Morcar.

Such angry prejudice 'gainst all things foreign,
Foreign alone because as yet unknown.
Nought is more baneful to our land and people
Than the complaining cry of discontent
For which there is no cause.

Harold (advancing).

But should it prove
There be a cause for it and a right good one?
(All turn in astonishment.)

Gytha.

Harold — thou here?

7

Harold (inclining his head to Edwin and Morcar).
> God greet ye honoured uncles!

(embracing his mother tenderly.)

My coming takes thee by surprise: did'st think
That I could fail thee on a day like this?

Gytha.

How, dost thou know then that the king comes hither?

Harold.

Therefore, well mindful of a vassal's duty
Thou see'st me here.

Edwin.
> And yet methinks t'were fitting

The vassal donned some richer dress than this
To give his Master welcome.

Harold.
> Twofold Reasons

Do urge me to retain this mourning dress.
Bright flaunting garments suit the Norman well,
For him t'is time of joy; the garb of mourning
Far better suits the Anglo-saxon.

Morcar.
> Nephew,

Loth should I be to find thee on the side
Of those who ever murmur and complain.

Harold.

Uncle, I fear that thou dost wrong the murmurers.

Morcar.

Thou, nephew Harold dost forget I fear
That I'm as old as now had been thy father,
And thou as old — as is thy father's son.

Harold.

T'is for this cause that on that side thou't find me
Where now would stand my father, did he live.

Morcar.

We'll further speak thereon at other time —
Know'st thou to what intent the king comes hither?

Harold.

Methinks he comes our loyalty to test,
If ready welcome to our home we give him?

Morcar.

Not that alone — he doth expect a guest,
William the Duke of Normandy comes hither.

(Harold, Gytha and Stigand, greatly agitated.)

Nay!

Morcar.
But it is so.

Harold.
But it dare not be!

Morcar.

Did I not think my news would set ablaze
Thy angry spirit. —

Harold.
Might I be accursed
If calmly I could listen to such tidings!
Thou, Uncle, thou, wert present on the day,
On which at Winchester my honoured father
Placed upon Edward's head the Saxon crown.
What was the solemn oath king Edward took

9

Upon that day? Why art thou silent Uncle?
Thou know'st the oath, for thou and all the nobles
Of our good Saxon people stood around him
As guardians of that oath! Most reverend bishop
I pray of thee, repeat to him the oath.

Stigand.

Before the face of God king Edward swore
That ne'er a Norman to this land he'd call.

Morcar.

All this I know right well.

Harold.

        Thou know'st it well
And yet dost think that I can calmly hear it,
When he himself doth bid the Duke come hither?

Morcar.

I said the Duke would wait upon the king.
Is that then being bidden?

Edwin.

        Shall they say
The Anglosaxons are the only people
Who nothing know of gentle courtesy?

Harold.

A curse upon the gloss of courtesy
If it be used as mantle to a crime!

Morcar.

Who speaketh here of crime?

10

Harold.

E'en I, mine Uncle!

The shepherd who doth ope the door himself
To give his flock unto the wolf —

Edwin.

What folly!

Harold.

Ay, ay, I'll sooner trust the hungry wolf
That prowls around the fold, than I'll believe
The Duke comes here as friend!

Morcar.

Now hear my words,

William is Edward's nephew — know'st thou that?
Good — Edward loves him — that, thou callest crime
That others would entitle human nature.
Edward has lands that lie in Normandy
Bequeathed him by his mother; know'st thou that?
Good — Until Edward's death, Duke William holds
These lands in fiefdom — after Edward's death
They are his own — hast thou well understood?
Duke William takes to-day the oath of fiefdom,
And this thou knowest must be done in person.
Now tell me, can there be in all the world
A simpler cause than this for William's coming?

Harold.

And should the reason for his coming seem
A hundred fold more innocent than this,
Admittance to my castle I'll deny him!

Morcar.

Thou wilt not?

Harold.

Ay, I will!

Edwin.

But should the king
Demand it of thee

Harold.

Still I would deny it
My gates I'd ope not to my country's foe
If God in heaven himself should bid me do so.

Morcar.

I pray thee cousin, bring thy son to reason!

Edwin (to Gytha).

He'll bring thee ruin with his foolish ravings!

Gytha.

Is it your will I speak? t'is good so hearken.
The words that unto ye my son hath spoken,
Were e'en as had they been mine own.

Morcar.

Thou'dst suffer -

Gytha.

Nay more than that: within his hand I lay
My fate and all that doth concern my house,
That he o'errule it: unto him I trust
The rudder, that the Pilot he may be,
Whose will, my will shall be where'er it guide
Amidst the billows of these stormy times.

(Enter **Attendant** from L.)

Pardon my lords, and my most noble lady,
Townsmen of Dover stand before the gates
And urgent beg admittance and a hearing.

G y t h a (gives a sign of assent).

A t t e n d a n t (opening door L).

(Enter **Ordgar**, his head bandaged. **Edric. Baldwulf. Wilfried.**)

E d w i n (to Ordgar).

What bringeth thee in such unsightly guise
Before us?

O r d g a r (his eyes glaring wildly).

How? unsightly? that may be —
God's punishment on those who thus have made it.

M o r c a r.

Who is this aged brawler?

G y t h a.

Err I not
Thy name is known to me: art thou not — Ordgar?

O r d g a r.

True noble dame and did thy husband live,
Who liveth now, alas, alas, no more,
He'd know me well!

M o r c a r.

Enough, enough, now say
What t'is thou wishest.

13

Ordgar.

Pardon, gracious Sir
If not in well set words I should express it
It is but one thing — but a thing so great —

Morcar.

Speak clearly, to the purpose.

Ordgar.

Give me time!
Would words but come! they lie upon my breast —
They seem to choke me —

Edwin.

Think'st thou we have time —

Ordgar.

Good, good, to make an end then with one word,
And that a holy one because t'was made
The first of days and with the first of men:
Justice! (raising his hands to heaven.)

Edric and Baldwulf.

Ay, Justice! Justice, noble lords!

Morcar.

Who did ye wrong?

Ordgar.

The Norman t'was that wronged us.

Morcar.

Ever the Norman!

Ordgar.

Gaze upon this brow
On which he wrote his name in bloody letters:
The ruthless peacebreaker!

14

Morcar.

What meaneth this?
We have no time to day to list to tales
Of idle brawlings — come to-morrow — hence! —

Ordgar.

How? Brawlings? How?

Edric.

Thy pardon gracious sir,
T'was an unheard of breaking of the peace.

Morcar.

May be: to-morrow we'll enquire further,
Go now!

Harold.

One word I pray thee.

Morcar.

To what end?

Harold (to the people).

Tell me of whom it is that ye complain?

Morcar (to Harold).

How now? How now? Hast thou not heard then Harold,
That I thine uncle, eldest of thy House
Refused a hearing?

Harold.

Earl Morcar remember,
It is not thou, t'is I am Earl of Dover.

Morcar.

This stripling's arrogance will turn his brain.

15

Harold.

Speak now old man.

Ordgar.

Ah gracious sir, this morn,
Count Eustace rode into the town of Dover
With fifty armed men.

Harold.

    And then what happened?

Ordgar.

Then, when the troop had reached the market place,
Down from his horse Count Eustace sprang, and called,
„Make quarters for the Duke and for our men
Amid these poodle-heads."

Harold.

    Well, Well, what further?

Ordgar.

Then as though Dover were a hostile town,
From every side they fell upon our houses,
Forcing the entrances with brutal might.

Harold.

Is't true?

Ordgar.

    Ay! Ay!

Edric and **Baldwulf.**

    As we ourselves have witnessed!

Ordgar.

And as the citizens their homes defended
From out their sheaths, their swords the Normans drew,

16

And — Ah! — I scarce can speak — a curse upon them —
In time of peace, good sir, in mid'st of peace —

Harold.

Speak calmly —

Ordgar.

Thirtycitizens of Dover
Lay slaughtered on the ground of Dover's streets.

Stigand.

May God protect us!

Gytha.

Most atrocious deed!

Harold.

How? thirty townsmen? slaughtered?

Edric (pointing to Wilfried).

This young priest,
Who late returned from Rome will say t'is true.

Harold to Wilfried).

This thou did'st see?

Wilfried.

Alas, good sir I saw it.

Harold.

Remember that thy lips to God are given.
Let then the words they speak be as the dove
That hovers o'er the Ocean of our passions —
Say not I saw, hast thou not clearly seen,
For bear'st thou witness to this old man's words —

Edwin.

Yes, truly if —

Harold.

Who speaks in Godwin's house
Till Godwin's heir doth ask him for his words?

(to Wilfried)

Once more I ask —

Wilfried.

May God in heaven forbid
That e'er again I see what I have seen.
May God forbid that e'er again I hear
The grewsome sound of sharp edged sword blades falling
With gashing, deadly strokes on human heads.

Harold.

And this thou saw'st, thou heardest?

Wilfried.

Every word
This old man spoke called up before my sight
A bloody picture tangible and fearful,
To haunt unceasingly each nightly dream.

Harold.

Now by the memory of my dead father.
Now by my mother and by all that's holy,
By all things that are sacred to my heart,
Before the king himself your cause I'll plead —

Morcar.

Consider Harold!

Harold.

Ay, I will consider,
How best to forge a word of such deep anguish,
That falling like a thunderbolt from heaven
It pierce 'it's way into the monarch's ear.
And rouse him with it's crash from that dull sleep
Into the which the norman tongues have lulled him.

Morcar (calling to I.).

Bid my atendants saddle quick the horses,
I have no more in common with this man.

Edwin.

I go with thee.

Harold.

To hell then with ye both!

Morcar.

That to thine uncle?

Harold.

Ay thou perjured saxon!
Betrayer of thy people and thy country!

Morcar (to Gytha).

Thou hear'st him?

Gythg.

Truly and my soul exults!
Harold my son, who till this very day,
Only by name as Godwin's son I've known,
Pride of my heart, most rare and precious gift
That unto me thy noble father gave:
All England gazes on thee through these eyes
Filled with maternal pride!

(she opens her arms widely).

Morcar.

Upon your heads then,
May fall the consequences of your ravings!
Earl Edwin come.

Harold (turning from them).

Go miserable threateners!

Morcar (leaving the Hall L.)

Thou shalt account for this.

Edwin.

Ay, ay, that shalt thou!
(Exeunt both L.)

Harold.

Ha! did but ev'ry Anglosaxon breast
Beat loud as ours, a tone would then ring forth,
So mighty that these frankish fooleries
Would die away as doth the tinkling bell
When from the lofty Dome the Chimes are pealing!
(a flourish of trumpets is heard.)

Gytha.

Hark, hark!

Stigand.

It is the trumpet of the Norman.

Harold.

Thus doth the Saxon king announce his coming.
How hard, how coldly rings the brazen metal!
It seems to call us unto strife and combat —
Ay call, thou'lt find me ready for the Fight!

(Enter a **Herald** from L.)

Edward the son of Ethelred, the Saxon king
Demands admittance into Dover castle.

Harold.

Say to the king that free is Dover castle
To every Saxon. — Wherefore dost thou linger?

Herald.

This is the answer?

Harold.

T'is!

Herald.

I haste to bring it!
(exit L.)

Stigand.

Harold, I would not have thee vex the king.
I fear t'will anger him that he should find
(pointing at the citizens).
These people with thee.

Harold.

Let these people stay,
For I will shew to him these visages
On each of which, as in an open book,
A tale of grief and misery stands written.
(pointing at Ordgar)
This hoary head, dyed by the Norman's hand
In bloody colours, shall he gaze upon

21

And see therein the grim, pale face of truth:
He who doth live but on the wily whisperings
Of Frankish sycophants!

Gytha.
        The king approaches.

(Enter from L. — **king Edward, Robert of Jumièges, Count Eustace of Boulogne, Odo** and **Randolf.** (All are attired in the Norman fashion.)
(Gytha and all present receive the king deferentially.)

Edward (to Gytha).
God greet thee, Countess.

Gytha.
        Welcome royal Sir
To Godwin's house.

Eustace (aside to Edward).
        Hast heard? How proud it sounds.
His house — methought t'was held in fiefdom?

Edward
(ascends the Dais and seats himself on the kind of throne placed upon it — the Normans stand in groups behind him.)

Edward
(gazing at the citizens)   (to those near him).
Who are these people that he has about him?

Robert (half audibly).
A common rabble.

Eustace (in a low tone).
        He's the peasant's king;
These are his courtiers.

Edward (aside).

How they glare upon me,
Dumb as the fishes — not a word of greeting!
The loathsome beings, well I know they hate me!
(aloud to Harold)
I see that thou hast guests!

Harold.

No, gracious sire.

Edward.

Thou sayest no, although thy guests I see?

Harold.

These are no guests my sovereign.

Edward.

What then are they?

Harold.

Poor folk are they, my gracious lord and king,
Who came to me complaining of their need.

Edward.

Who suffers need within my realm?

Ordgar.

We suffer.

Edward.

Why come ye not to me then, to your king?
Why go ye unto others?

Ordgar.

Why? —

23

Edward.

I know ye!
Ye do not trust me! Why? Am I of stone?
Trust me ye shall! I'll have it so!

Harold.

They trust thee!

Edward.

Duke, speak not that which thou dost not believe.

Harold.

My gracious sovereign, if thou wilt permit me —
These men are citizens of Dover —

Edward.

Dover?

Harold.

Ay, just as I, thou know'st, am Earl of Dover.

Robert (to the king).

Let him account for that!

Eustace (as above).

Bethink the shame!

Edward (turning toward them).

Your help I need not. (aloud) Duke I much do fear
That with a punishment I must begin
My visit to thee.

Harold.

How?

24

Edward.

Thou wilt have heard
Of the affront that Dover put upon me?

Harold.

On thee? affront?

Edward.

Through those whom I sent hither,
To whom when coming in their sovereigns name,
Seeking for quarters for the Norman Duke,
(Who as thou know'st is nephew to their king)
Most boorishly such quarters were refused.

Harold.

Thou art in earnest?

Edward.

If thou deem'st I jest
Plainly I'll shew how earnest is my meaning.

Harold.

That would I beg of thee — for Sire I fear
It is an earnest matter —

Edward.
Truly —

Harold.

And so grave,
That all the humour of thy frankish lords
Will fail to make it fitting cause for laughter.

Edward.

What tone is this?

Harold.

The tone —

Edward (to Gytha).

      I trust my lady
Thy son forgetteth not his monarch's presence.

Gytha.

He is of age my king.

Citizens.

     Long live the Countess!

Edward.

Ay, though the rabble tenfold shout approval
Thou darest not forget I am thy king!

Eustace.

I pray thee grant me speech!

Harold.

     Ay let him speak,
For he will tell of the heroic deeds
That he has done against defenceless men
In Dover's streets!

Eustace.

     Ha! wert thou not a Saxon
Who nothing knows of knightly courtesy
An answer I would give thee —

Harold.

     In it's stead
Mark thou the oath I take, infernal Norman,
That when and where in open field we meet,

26

Will I, with thirty Anglosaxon blows
Write on thy back in letters clear the names
Of those same thirty citizens thou'st slaughtered.

Ordgar.

God bless our Duke!

Edric and Baldwulf.

God bless our young Duke Harold!

Edward (restraining Eustace).

Count of Boulogne, all that which thou hast told me
In answer to my questions on this matter,
That truly happened? Neither more nor less?

Eustace.

Most truly, Sire.

Harold.

Count of Boulogne, thou liest!

Normans.

Down with this poodle-headed Saxon, down!

Ordgar.

Dare to lay hand upon him dastard Norman!

Harold.

Peace, peace, old man — my gracious lord and king,
I know my anger makes my tongue too swift —
With due submission bend I down before thee
And pray thee, hear these people.

Edward.

Hear what people?

Harold (drawing Ordgar forward).

Gaze on this aged man — see how his blood
With darkly crimson, hot, reproachful eye
Glances from out the bandage — he is townsman
In the same land where thou art king! the Normans
Have done this deed.

Edward (turning away).

        No blood — I'll see no blood!

Harold.

Yet thousand, many thousand bloody tears
Are flowing in thy land! these thou must see!

Eustace.

'Tis I who take this blood upon my soul,
Wholely and solely rest this deed on me.

Stigand.

Thou over-daring man —

Edward.

        Methinks, good bishop
Thou ow'st me thanks that I permit thy presence,
Let me not hear thy voice.

(a flourish of trumpets is heard)

        Who cometh hither?

(Enter a **Norman Herald** from L.)

Herald.

Unto the royal Edward, Saxon king,
William, the Duke of Normandy brings greeting.

The Normans.

Hail to our Duke!

28

Eustace.

Permit us, gracious Sire
With fitting courtesy to bid him welcome.

Edward (pointing towards Gytha and Harold).

We are the guests — here stand our host and hostess.
I pray thee Countess, go receive the Duke.

Gytha.

Ask thou my son, the master of the castle.
(pause.)

Eustace (to Harold).

How long shall stand our master at thy gate?

Harold.

As long as I remain this castle's master.

Eustace (to Edward).

Thou heard'st him — Sire I pray thee give us leave
To bid Duke William welcome.
(the Normans descend from the dais.)

Harold (placing himself before them).

I forbid it!
(The Normans shew signs of agitation.)

Edward.

He has not understood me — hear, Duke Harold,
Thy king doth beg thee —

Harold.

I refuse him!

Edward.

Harold!

Stigand (to Harold).

In this one matter yield thy will to his.

Edward.

Methought thou wast not born within a stable.
Dost nothing know of courtesy and manners?

Harold.

For human beings there are higher laws
Than courtesy.

Edward.

Thy son is raving, Countess.
Think of the shame that he doth put upon me:
The Duke comes here to take the oath of fiefdom
Anent his heritance in Normandy.
Shall then a vassal of my realm refuse
The very thing I gave my royal word
That I would grant him?

Gytha (pointing at Harold).

Yonder stands my Lord,
His word is mine, and mine too his resolve.

Edward.

Perverted, haughty, most rebellious race!
Once more bethink ye!

Harold.

First do thou remember
Thy vow upon thy coronation day!

30

Ordgar.

Thy holy vow!

Citizens.

Thy vow at Winchester!

Edward.

God is my witness that t'is ye compel me.

Harold.

Thou perjured man call thou not God to witness!

Edward.

Perjured! And that to me? To me thy king?

Harold.

Ay to thy very face, thou rotten branch
Upon the ancient tree of Saxon Kings!

Stigand.

Harold — by God — bethink!

Harold.

Nay, let me speak!
Now mark thou how these frail and weary limbhs
Will bend beneath him, if upon his head
I pour but half the Misery he hath heaped
Upon each Saxon breast — Ay to thy face
Thou puppet of the Normans —

Robert.

Dost thou hear him?

Edward.

Ah who will save me from this raving madman?

31

Eustace.

Sire that will we: Ho Normans! to the king!

(Normans appear at the doors R. and L. with drawn Swords.)
(a gloomy pause.)

Edward (rises).

Ye all have heard the words this man hath spoken?

The Normans.

We heard them.

Edward.

    Heard — how he upon mine honour
Did cast the stigma of his traiterous words —
How to my face, he shamelessly refused
Th'Obedience that as vassal he doth owe me,
Thus hindering me to hold my given word.
Bear witness, all of ye to this!

The Normans.

        We do!

Edward.

Harold the son of Godwin, I declare
Forfeit of goods and lands. Banished, I grant him
Three days of respite, counting from to-day,
But if upon the fourth day I should meet him,
His head shall fall beneath the hangman's hand.

(Murmurings amongst the people)

Why do the people murmur at my words?

Ordgar.

The hangman thou can'st seek across the sea!

Edward.

I'or this shalt thou account! Yet of my mercy
Thou Countess mayest remain in Dover Castle.

Gytha (with a bitter laugh).

Thou? Of thy mercy? thou?

Edward.

What means this laughter?

Gytha.

Shew mercy unto those, thou dar'st to punish.

Edward.

Thou'lt have no mercy?

Gytha.

Shame thou not this word,
The fairest ornament of manly power,
Thou weakling to whom fear alone gives strength!
Go, bring my Wulfnoth hither Bishop —

(Stigand ex·t R.)

Learn
O most unkingly man, from us now learn
The noble language royal blood doth speak.
And should I go from hence unto the scaffold,
My head beside his head I'd gladly lay.
Upon that day of Winchester I stood
And saw how Godwin made yon man a king
And by my sons fair curling locks I swear
My heart was then not half so light and gay
As t'is to-day when reft of home and rights
My sons I follow into banishment.

(Stigand comes from R. with Wulfnoth).

Stigand.
I bring to thee the child.

Gytha.
            Come, Wulfnoth, come.
Thus with my sons enfolded in mine arms
I call unto the mothers in all England;
Can one of ye be happier than I?

(She places one arm round Harold's neck and presses Wulfnoth to her side.)

Ordgar.
Not one, great countess!

Harold.
          Come, we will from hence.
Where might prevaileth, right must hold it's peace.

(to Edward)

At parting, the inheritance I leave thee
Of sleepless hours in wakeful, endless nights,
Filled with the groanings of a troubled conscience,
By day the aspect of a murmuring people,
And night and day the trembling and the terror
Of the approaching hour —

Eustace.
What hour mean'st thou?

Harold
(raises his hand with a threatening gesture and turns with his mother and Wulfnoth
towards R. to leave the hall).

Robert (to Edward).
Take thou an hostage from them.

ACT 1.

Edward.

How — an hostage?

Robert.

Demand her youngest son.

Edward.

I'm loth to do so.

Eustace.

And yet t'is needful.
(aloud)
Countess, hold, the king
Hath somewhat yet to say to thee.
(all turn back.)

Edward.

Ay Countess Gytha,
It pains me — yet I need thy youngest son
As hostage.

Gytha.

How? this child? this tender child?

Edward.

Yes, for his elder brothor's evil will.

Gytha.

To leave my child! Ah slay me then at once,
Not limb for limb!

Eustace (seizes Wulfnoth roughly).

T'is not thy life we'd have,
It is the boy.

Wulfnoth (struggling).

Ah, help me, brother Harold!

Harold (tearing the child from the grasp of Eustace.

Ye shall not take the child!

(The men in arms advance several steps nearer from R. and L. Harold glances round him, shakes his head angrily and turns to the king.)

By God in heaven
Who seeth all that thou this day mayest do,
Swear that no hurt shall happen to the boy.

Edward.

No hurt shall happen to him — that I promise.

Harold (raising Wulfnoth and pressing him to his breast).

Courage my brother; we shall meet again.

(he sets the boy down.)

Embrace thy mother.

(to Gytha.)

Mother, at this hour
Be brave!

Gytha.

Be brave! — ah yes — I will — I will —
My child — my darling —

Wulfnoth.

Mother —

Gytha.

Do not speak,
For if I hear thy voice my child — my child —

(she sinks down suddenly before the child and strains it convulsively to her breast.)

What dark foreboding fills my shuddering soul:
Ah, never shall I see this child again!

Harold.

Thou shalt — I swear it.

Gytha (to Edward).

Edward, keep thy wolves
Far from my lamb: for this to thee I say,
Whoe'er be cause that I this child shall lose,
Shall scorch and wither 'neath my deadly hate!
Shall sink beneath my fury! By my curse,
Shall he be driven from the throne of grace
Upon the judgement day! — My child, my child,
That I must clothe thine innocent young life
In such an armour of unholy curses. —

(she rises).

Harold, come hence with me, I will not weep
Before these demons — guard thou well my child!
Once I shall ask it of thee — Wulfnoth — No! —
Now must I go — now, now or nevermore —
Hence — look not back at him — away, away.

(Harold supporting Gytha leaves the Hall — the Citizens follow them slowly to R.)

The Curtain falls.

End of the first Act.

Act 2.

Scene 1.

(A park at Rouen) a flowery thicket. Toward the front R. a grassy mound over-shadowed by a rosebush in full bloom. As the curtain rises horns are heard behind the stage.)

(Enter **Adéle. Alice. Eleanor. Pages** from R.)

Adéle.

O Alice, Eleanor, beloved maidens,
Was ever morn so bright and fair as this?
The sun has fall'n in love with its own heaven,
Heaven with the earth —

Alice.

            To make the matter short,
Ever the same old song of loved and loving.

Eleanor.

Poor Alice sighs — Adéle fairest queen
Of forest and of meadow, mighty mistress
That rulest o'er my heart, what dost thou purpose
That we this day together shall achieve?

Adéle.

Let us hold council!

(she sits down on the grassy mound, Alice lies at her feet, Eleanor remains standing.)

38

Eleanor.

Thou shalt be Diana,
And we, like Atalanta, robed for hunting
Will follow thee through wooded glen and mead.

Adéle.

And what says Alice?

Alice.

Eleanor may hunt,
I know of somewhat better.

Eleanor.

She'll advise thee,
That resting here beneath this bush of roses
We listen to the nightingales: see, see,
How her fair head o'erfilled with gentle dreamings
Bends like a rose weighed down with heavy dew.

Alice.

Would it not pleasure thee to test the jennet
Thy father gave to thee?

Adéle.

Ah, wondrous well!
Ye both ride with me?

Eleanor.

I will take the chestnut!

Alice.

And I will ride the grey.

Adéle (turns to her attendants).

Come hither, page

(page approaches.)

Order our horses to be brought! and — listen —
Prepare my falcon, set him on his hood.

Page.

I haste Princess — which falcon shall I bring,
Is it thy will I bring thee the Norwegian?

Adéle.

No, no, the one my father gave me.

Page.

Pardon,
They both are from the Duke!

Adéle.

Ah yes, t'is true!
And what have I that doth not come from him,
My noble father? Fortunate Adéle!
The Iceland Falcon with the raven plumage
And snowy breast, that bring to me — the other
Bring to my Eleanor, my well loved friend.

(Page exit.)

Eleanor.

Dear Mistress, thou dost well deserve thy bliss,
For all thou would'st make happy.

(kisses her hand.)

Adéle.

On the way
Alice must tell to us some wondrous tale
Of Arthur's Court.

Eleanor.
                    And of his gallant knights
Of Lancelot.

Adéle.
And of fair Melusina.

Alice.
I think ye've plundered me of all my treasures;
I know nought more.

Eleanor.
                    Dear lady, dost believe her?

Adéle.
No Eleanor, but poets and story tellers
Must be, like birds, with tempting sweetmeats fed.
The gentle dreams that dwell within their souls
We draw with flattery soft unto the threshhold.
                    (she embraces Alice.)
Come lady Stubborn, name to me the price
Thou'lt have for being gracious?

Alice.
                    Sweetest mistress,
Of all princesses, dearest, kindest, best!
This dainty morsel t'is, for which I'll ever
Do all thou willst.
                    (kisses her lips.)

Page *(returning).*
                    Princess, the horses wait,
As thou commandest —

Adéle.

Up into the saddle!
Had I but wings that grew upon my shoulders,
Then with my Falcon would I seek the skies!

(Adele, Alice and Eleanor are hastily leaving the stage L.)

(at the same moment enter **William**, the **Seneschal, Barons** from L.)

(William advances toward Adele and catches her in his arms.)

William.

Hold, hold wild falcon fly not yet away!
Thy father needs his daughter here on earth.

Adéle.

My father, home from England?

William.

As thou seest.

Adele (embracing him).

Welcome, most welcome my much-honoured Master!

William.

Thine honoured master! List to this bold child,
How it doth dare to mock it's father's weakness.

Adéle.

But art thou not the stern and mighty Duke
Before whose face both low and lofty tremble?

William.

To others I may be so — but to thee?

⊸ ACT 2. ⊶

Adéle.

O, for an orator, from whom to learn
How to give fitting answer to this question.
My own, my dear, my well-beloved father!
<small>(kissing him.)</small>

William.

My blossom bright, my breath of morning air
Amid the dusty workaday of life:
How fared it with my daughter in mine absence?

Adéle.

Well, for thy heart remained here with me.
Did'st thou not miss it father, yon in England?

William.

I missed it not, because I had thee still
And yet in England left thee.

Adéle.
How so, father?

William.

Come, look thou here, dost thou not miss the chain,
From off my neck, on which thy picture hung
In golden setting?

Adéle.
Ay — where hast thou left it?

William.

With thy great uncle, Edward, England's king.
I shewed thy picture to him, when he saw it,
No more he'd part from it.

Adéle.

So help me heaven —
I've heard he counteth nigh on seventy years,
Is that the bridegroom thou for me hast chosen?

William (solemnly).

Not so, and yet I went to seek a bride:
I was the bridegroom and the bride I found,
Is called „England"!

Seneschal.

Ha! that meaneth —

William.

Barons,
In shortest space, the aspect of the world
Will much be changed from that it wears to-day.
Know all — King Edward with a solemn vow
Appointed me as heir upon his death.

Seneschal.

Thou as his heir?

William.

As heir unto his crown,
When Edward dies, t'is I am king of England.

Seneschal.

Star of the Normans may I see that day!
King Edward swore it?

William.

With a sacred vow,
Ask our Archbishop, Robert of Jumièges,
He heard it.

Barons.

Hail to William, king of England!

William (to Adéle).

What says Adéle, royal child of England
To such bright picture of the future?

Adéle.

Nought.

William.

Nought? That upon thy fair young brow
A royal diadem thy father places?

Adéle.

The skies of England I have heard are grey
In Normandy far rather would I rest.

Seneschal (glances behind the scene L.).

Pardon the question, my most gracious Duke
Who is this child that thou hast brought with thee
From England?

William.

Now, by all the saints above
Almost I had forgotten him: where bides he?

Seneschal (pointing to L.).

Here — overcome with weariness and sleep.

(Enter a Norman baron, who carries the sleeping Wulfnoth
in his arms from L.).

Adéle.

O, Alice, Alice, see what cometh hither!
Say did'st thou ever see a thing so fair?

Alice (advancing to look at the child).

Ah, what a lovely child!

Adéle.

       Hush! do not wake him!
See how his rosy cheeks are flushed with sleep,
And O, these locks — like threads of brightest gold —
Ah, what a beauteous child!

William.

       But hearken daughter,
Thou must not lose thy heart to this young fellow —
He is my prisoner.

Adéle.

       Prisoner — this child?
Thou'st not in earnest father?

William.

       Never more so.
As hostage, Edward took him from his mother,
And from his brother, the rebellious Harold
Who dwelleth now in Flanders, and the child
To me was trusted for his safer keeping.

Adéle.

So poor in years and yet so rich in sorrow?
Still, still, he's waking.

Wulfnoth (awaking).

       Mother dear — where art thou?
Where is my brother Harold?

William.

Set him down.

(Wulfnoth is placed upon the ground.)

Come little Wulfnoth, come and give thy hand —

Wulfnoth (turning to go).

I'll to my mother —

Seneschal (holding him back and laughing).

Bide a while, young sir!

Adéle.

Be not so rough with him! kneeling down by him.)

My darling tell me,
Art thou afraid of me?

Wulfnoth.

No — thou art good —
But he — (pointing of William) is cruel.

Adéle.

No, that is he not.
See dear one, as art thou thy mother's child,
E'en so am I the child of yonder man.

(Wulfnoth puts his arms round Adéle's neck and cries bitterly.)

God comfort thee poor tender little heart.

(she' rises.)

I pray thee father trust the boy to me,
Refuse me not:

William.

That may not be, Adéle.
Thou hearest he was given me as hostage.

Adéle.

Ah see this childish face all wet with tears
Turning it's glance complainingly to nature
To seek it's rights of her, to seek for love;
O father, who with love so deep and great
Dost fill each hour of thine own child's life,
Thou can'st not be the man who would deprive
This child of it's sweet rights — if thy Adéle.
In stranger's hands —

William.

      Away with such wild fancies!
I will not hear them.

Adéle.

      Severed from thy side
In distant dungeon pined and wept for thee?

William (pressing Adéle passionately to his Breast).

Thou, severed from my side? take, take the child —
But guard him well for me.

Adéle.

      Beloved father,
I'll guard him as the light of mine own eyes!
    (to Wulfnoth)
Come little one — come — Wulfnoth — so thou'rt called?

(Enter **Montgomery** to the former).

Montgomery.

Important news from Flanders, gracious Duke;
Harold, with twenty ships, that he collected
Set forth for England.
    (great agitation.)

Wiliam.
,S' death! — when happened this?

Montgomery.
Three days ago t'is said he put to sea.

William.
This day his ships may sail upon the Thames?

Montgomery.
That well may be.

Seneschal.
Then woe unto king Edward!
The coasters and the citizens of London
Will arise in to a man bold rebellion
So soon they see his banner waving.

William.
Hasten,
We will send messengers across the sea.

(he turns to leave the stage but once more approaches Adéle, who with Alice
and Eleanor is occu-pied about Wulfnoth.)

Harold, thou son of Godwin, have a care
For if thou troublest me —

Adéle.
O father! father!
How fearful are thy looks!

William.
My child, remember,
Upon this earth, there lives one man alone
With power to harm me, and that one is Harold.
The heart of th'enemy is in thy hands,
Solemn the gift that unto thee I trust.

Adéle (pressing Wulfnoth closely to her side).

Be still my little one I will not leave thee.

(Transformation.)

Scene 2.

(A room in the palace of London. Doors R. — L. C. (a few steps lead up to the centre door, before which a curtain is hung).

(Enter **Robert of Jumièges** — **Eustace of Boulogne** from R.)

Eustace.
How stands the matter? Hath king Edward signed?

Robert.
Not yet.

Eustace.
Not yet? and will he sign at all?

Roberf.
As soon a he's another than he is.
Ten times the sentence has been laid before him —
Ten times he said, the case he'd well consider
And twenty times he has refused to sign it.
It maddens one to serve a man like this.

Eustace.
Thou know'st that Harold stands before the gates.
Within these very walls ferments rebellion
And sullen anger broods in every soul.
This day those Dover citizens must die,
One firm, unflinching bloody deed alone,
That changes love to deep and abject terror,
Can save us yet.

Robert.

All this I know is true.
But from that hour, when Edward to our Duke
Hath promised England, he detests the Normans.

Eustace.

Out on this perfect model of all weakness
That rues to-day the deed of yesterday!
Tell him it is a question of his life.

Robert.

He'll say it is a means weve used too often.

Eustace.

Too oft! too oft! Ay, ay the only weapon
That nature gave to cowards is — mistrust.

Robert
(going to the door c. L. lifting the curtain.)

I hear the king approaching, step aside.

Eustace.

T'is well, thou'lt find me in the antichamber.
But see that he delay not with the sentence,
I feel my patience is but short of breath.
(exit R.)

Robert.

I'll tear the sentence from his very soul.

(Enter **king Edward** leaning on **Wilfried**. (he holds a scroll in his hand
— advances through the centre —).

Robert (going toward him).
Thou'st signed the sentence my most gracious Sire?

Edward (gazing alternately at Robert and Wilfried).
Your countenances I would fain compare —
(to Wilfried)
Thon art a Saxon?

Wilfried.
Yes my gracious king.

Edward (to Robert).
And thou a Norman?

Robert.
As thou knowest Sire.

Edward.
There's somew hat of the hawk about thy visage,
As t'is with all thy people.

Robert.
Gracious Sire
Give me the sentence, if thou now hast signed it.

Edward.
E'en as the hawk he swoops upon his prey —

Robert.
Give me the sentence for the time is pressing.

Edward.

The time is pressing — ah the cursed time!
Say, art thou not a priest of that mild Saviour
Who died in love to us?

Robert.

      I am — thou know'st il.

Edward.

Wert thou a priest of God, woud'st thou not shudder
At such a bloody page of direful import?

Robert.

Truly I shudder: but the voice of duty
O'ertones my horror.

Edward.

      Speak thou not so coldly.
A precious stone is duty yet it grows
In cruel hands, as flinty as the rock
That crushing, falls upon our fellowbeings!
Here written, stand the names of thirty men —
Bethink, these thirty men have thirty wives —
Each of these thirty men was as a tree
On which fair blossoms grew — these men have children —
And now a single word from out my lips
Like breath of pestilence shall waft grim murder
O'er all these lives. — And thou - ah hear'st thou not
What wailing tones of misery and anguish
Resound from out this scroll? O ye are wise:
Me, do ye place between yourselves and God —
My soul alone, upon the last great day
Shall bloodstained stand, before the mighty Judge! —

Robert.

Unjust the judge who sheweth too great mildness.
They fell upon thy kinsman with their weapons —
T'is they must perish, if thou'rt willed to live.

Edward.

But thirty — thirty — was enquiry made
Of all that on that day in Dover chanced?

Robert.

Most surely — and one other thing I'd tell thee
That first I heard to-day: the young Duke Harold
Doth march against thee with a powerful host.

Edward.

Harold! —

Robert.

        Doth stand now before London's walls;
With thundering blows he knocks at London's gates
And thousand rebel voices from within
Shout with grim welcome „enter, Harold, enter“.
Know'st thou the goal toward which his arm is stretched?
It is the crown of gold upon thy head!

Edward (laughing cunningly).

That were a pity.

Robert.

        What were pity, Sire?

Edward.

If Harold, with this one foolhardy stroke
The fair plans of your master should destroy?
O ye much troubled ones — how well I know ye!

Robert.

Unheard of! Thus to mock the man who saved thee!
Should Harold's mother fan with angry words
His rage against thee? Should she now demand
The child thou can'st not give her?

Edward.

        Ha! the child! — ,
Who was it councilled me to keep the child?
Who was it?   Well ye've snared me in your nets!

Robert.

Leave what is past, bethink thee of the present.

Edward.

Come hither — lay thy hand upon this scroll —
(Robert takes one side of the scroll, Edward holding the other.)

Behold t'is thus I share with thee this deed.
Take half the honour if it honour bring,
And half the curse — nay, all the curse be thine
If curse it bring.

Robert.

      On my head rest the curse!
(ho seizes the paper and goes out hastily with it.)

Edward.

God grant I shed not blood that's innocent!
I know none goeth sinless through the world,
But to shed blood — as long as I remember,
Never could I conceive how men could murder!
Murder — what tone within this word doth lie,
As t'were the vault of death itself did open
To shew to us the haunt of utter terror. —

55

Blood — human blood — what riddle deep in horror
Lies hidden 'neath this murky, crimson stream —
My lifeblood curdles see I human gore —
God in thy mercy, let these men be guilty,
That I may be no murderer — Ha! none here?
No living soul — (percieves Wilfried).

     Ah, thou art here my son, —
I'm glad — thy countenance doth please me well.
And thou hast been in Rome? I pray thee tell me —
Of yonder azure skies for I have heard
They are not grey and leaden as are ours. —

Wilfried.

I cannot tell thee now of holy Rome
My heart is torn within me! Ah, those men —

Edward.

The thirty?

Wilfried.

    Ay — who all this day must die.
Did'st thou but know the immeasurable anguish —

Edward.

I know it!

Wilfried.

   No — thou saw'st not what I saw!

Edward (with terrified looks).

A something warns me — that I should not ask thee
What t'is thou'st seen? What saw'st thou?

Wilfried.

That e'en,
Which chanced in Dover when —

Edward.

Thou — thou hast seen it?

Wilfried.

I saw it all my gracious Sire. —

Edward.

Still — still!
For in thine eyes I see it clearly written —
Those deeds — were not — as they were told to me?

Wilfried.

Ah no, t'was not the truth thy told thee, sire —
The Normans, felling all things with their swords
With violence forced entrance in the houses,
And slaughtered thirty citizens of Dover!

Edward (laughing wildly).

And therefore is it that the Saxon king
Sends thirty after them to please the Normans!
(The tolling of a muffled bell is heard.)

Wilfried.

Pray Sire — o pray to God for these men's souls —
Hear'st thou? the gloomy bell doth toll their sentence.

Edward.

Cain slew but one man — thirty do I murder!
Gaze not upon me — turn away — but no —
Go, bid them hold!

Wilfried.
        Ah, Sire it is too late.

Edward.
Too late — the air is full of direful groans —
Hark how the bell is tolling Murder, Murder!
It is a people that doth curse it's king.

        (Enter **Stigand** in haste from L.)

Stigand.
King of the Saxons — I'st by thy command,
These thirty citizens are led to death?
Men wholly innocent?

Edward.
                By my command,
The Normans bade me do it.

Stigand.
                Ah, my king
I hear thy heart is stranger to this matter;
Swift — give a counterorder!

Edward.
        T'is too late.

Stigand.
Not yet - not yet — there is one man among us
With power to save them.

Edward.
        Name him!

S t i g a n d.

Should I do so?
Wilt thou then cast all rage and anger from thee?

E d w a r d.

Tell me his name and to my ears t'will sound
As t'were my Saviour's! Let me hear his name!

S t i g a n d.

Duke Harold stands before the walls of London;
Bid thou that London's gates to him be opened,
Give me the order, through the streets I'll hasten
And all the strength, a long and toilsome life
Hath left unto these weak and aged lungs,
I'll spend in one loud cry that all shall hear,
King Edward calleth Harold into London. —
Then to a man the people will arise
Like a fierce hurricane against the Norman,
And the doomed thirty citizens are free!

E d w a r d.

I know that when he cometh he will slay me,
Yet will I bless him, if he sets them free,
And freeth thus my soul from shedding blood!
Open the gates', call Harold into London!

S t i g a n d.

Haste checks my words — fare well my king, fare well!
(hastens out L.)

E d w a r d (to Wilfried).

Gaze not upon me with such hollow eyes,
Thou wonderest there are beings such as I,

For thou art young and youth is harsh in judgement,
Too swift — not just — and this thou knowest not,
That the same law that placed t'wixt day and night
The twilight, doth e'en so, hold good for men.
That there are beings neither light nor darkness,
But ever as the ausk.

Wilfried.

    Ah me — such beings
Must surely be of all the most unhappy.

(Enter **Robert, Eustace, Odo, Randolf,** hurriedly from L. Bishop
Stigand is dragged in after them).

Robert.

Here with him! Here! bring hither the false priest!
Where are the witnesses against this man?

Eustace.

I am the witness and denounce him forfeit
Of body, blood and life for foulest treason!
Plainly I heard him with these very ears
Inciting London's people to rebellion.
Deny it if thou can'st!

Stigand.

    Why that deny
Which fills my soul with pride.

Eustace.

    Archbishop Robert,
Pronounce his sentence.

Edward (ascending the steps before Door C.).

Hold, thou overbold one!
Dost thou not see the judge?

Eustace.

Pronounce the sentence!

Edward.

Once more I ask of thee if thou dost see me?

Eustace (with a menacing gesture).

One do I see for whom it were far better
I saw him not.

Edward.

Thou darest thus to speak?
Dar'st thus to threaten? Say how t'was with Dover?

Eustace.

Who speaketh now of Dover? Mark thee well
How traitors must be punished.   Be prepared.
(he draws his sword and approaches Stigand.)

Stigand.

What means thy sword?

Eustace.

This sword? It means thy life!

Edward.

Not yet enough of human blood?

Eustace.

Not yet!

The head upon these shoulders is but useless
Since nought it plots but treason and rebellion.
Yet severed from it's body it can serve me:
I'll cast it to the rabble as an answer
To prove how little t'is the Norman fears thee.

Stigand (flying to Edward).

Ah gracious Sire protect me from his fury.

Edward.

The king of England doth protect this man,
Who dare to lay a hand upon him?

Eustace.

I!

For England's rightful master I will slay him.

Edward.

Whom call'st thou England's rightful Master?

Eustace.

William,

The Duke of Normandy, my noble Lord!

Edward.

Thou scorpion that lay nestled 'neath my feet,
Lurking and lowering till the hour should come
For thee to sting me! wherefore went'st thou not
With thy dear master back to Normandy,
That in the ocean's depths thou hadst been buried?

Eustace (approaching Edward).

So doth it stand with us? Hence, hence the mask
That all too long impatiently I've worn:
Know that I hate thee, thou mistake of nature
That by an error made of thee a man.
Here have I rested as my master's steward,
And his inheritance I will protect
So surely as a Norman mother bore me
And no flat footed Anglosaxon woman!

(Enter a **Norman herald** in breathless haste).

Herald.

Fly, fly my lords! they burst the castle gates!

Robert.

Who storms the palace?

Herald.

              Harold is in London!

Stigand.

My God I thank thee!

Herald.

              On his milk white steed
He chargeth onwards — following on his traces,
As though the stones upon the streets of London
Were changed to heads, a human sea rolls on.
The pris'oners he delivered! they are free!

Eustace.

A pest upon him!

Edward.

     And the thirty live?
Have thanks, have thanks, thou Saviour of my soul!

Robert.

This is thine answer to these tidings? this?

Edward.

Robert I shewed thee once the secret passage
Beside the Thames — go, take the fleetest steeds
From out my stable, mount them swift and flee!

Robert.

The church of God goes forth from out this land
Deceived, betrayed by this country's king.
I Robert the Archbishop call aloud
To all who name themselves the Church's sons
That they shall place themselves upon my side.

   (Wilfried crosses over to him.)

Edward (to Wilfried)

Go not my son, it is not for thy weal!

Wilfried.

Yet I must go he is the priest of God,
And I as deacon am to him appointed.

Robert.

A curse on all that are not on my side
Hence hence Count Eustace!

   (Robert, Wilfried and the Normans exeunt C.)

Eustace.

    Nay I will not flee
Before this youthful boorish peasant-king!
A plan so full of spirit — courage — fire
In Vulcan's glowing smithy hotly forged,
To be worked out by the bold God of deeds,
Destroyed by such a wight! Who dares to hinder,
That I should hew him in a thousand pieces?

   (rushes upon Edward with drawn sword.)

(Enter **Harold** from R. — springs upon Eustace and holds back his raised arm).

Harold.

Harold, the Saxon!

Eustace. (furiously).

    Harold the accursed!

Harold (seizing his sword).

Hence with the sword from out this trait'rous hand!
Down to the very dust with this bold brow!

Edward (covering his eyes with his hand).

No blood before mine eyes! no blood! no blood!

Eustace (tearing himself from Harold's greep).

If I must flee before thy houndish pack —
At parting take from me the bitterest curse,
That e'er was fashioned in the flames of hell!

   (he flees through Door C.)

Harold.

Edward I swore to thee I would return;
Here at thy feet, my given word I cast
With ringing sound.

(Throws the Count's sword before Edward's feet.)

(Enter **Ordgar, Edric, Baldwulf** and **other citizens** from L.
carrying axes.)

The Citizens.

Destroy the hornet's nest!

Ordgar.

Hail Harold, son of Godwin!

Citizens.

Hail Deliverer!

Ordgar.

Ha we have come too late! From hence they fled!
Death, death to the Protector of the Normans!

(he swings his Axe against Edward.)

Citizens.

Down with him to the ground!

Ordgar.

First give us answer;
Who maketh good the terror we have suffered?
The rope around our necks? The foul disgrace
That on our heads with all too ready zeal
Was heaped, from day to day?

Citizens.

Destroy him! Vengeance!

66

Stigand.

Peace, peace ye ravers!

Edward.

     Bishop let them rave —
T'is not so hard to die as t'is to kill.
Harold I know full well thy stern resolve
Calls like the chime of death unto my life;
The eventide is come. — Here in the sight
Of these same thirty men that thou hast saved
I thank thee for thy deed.

(turning away toward R.)

Harold.

     My lord and king
Where goest thou?

Edward.

    Whereever thou dost send me.

Harold.

In all due reverence I do beseech thee:
Keep thou the throne that is thine own by right.

Edward.

Is this a dream? Harold, these words have sprung
From out thine heart?

Harold.

     By the almighty God,
Aud from it's very best and purest depths.

67

Edward.

O Harold — thou compellest me as beggar
To stand before thee only to receive.
Thou bringest tears unto these aged eyes?

Citizens.

His penance!

Harold.

Peace — no more; is not this visage
All stained with bitter tears enough of Penance?

Ordgar.

Master — thou know'st, he placed us neath the gallows

Citizens.

And, Life for Life!

Stigand.

Beneath the very heaven
That solemnly looks down upon this hour,
I'was he that tore ye from the hangman's hands,
I'was he that called Duke Harold into London.

Ordgar.

This were the truth? —

Stigand.

Behold my hoary head
Standing as warder upon life's last threshold
To warn me'against falsehood. T'is the truth.

Harold.

I cast all strife and conflict of the past.
Into oblivion's fathomless abyss
Hail to king Edward!

(kisses Edward's hand.)

Citizens.
Hail the Saxon king!

Edward (weeping).

Wonder not — mock not, that ye see me weep.
These tears alas, most bitterly reproach
A life that dragged me joyless and unloved
Through desert places. Most unhappy Edward,
And must thy life sink down to shades of even
Before it dare to hear the voice of love?

Stigand (looking L.).
Place for the Countess!

(Enter **Gytha** from L.).

Citizens.
Hail Duke Harold's mother!

Herold (going towards her).
Mother, thou comest at a happy hour;
Join in our festival.

Gytha.
My lord and king,
Thou surely wilt forgive a mother's heart
If it at first, in all the wealth of joy
Think of the treasure that alone it misses.
(pause.)
I pray thee Edward give me back my child.

Edward.
Believe me noble lady t'is well cared for.

Gytha.

I pray thee Sire, my child.

Edward.

He is not here.

Gytha.

Not here? Where is my child?

Edward.

Thou wilt be angry —
He is with William in the Norman's Land.
Believe me Lady, he is kind to children.

Gytha.

How say'st thou? Wulfnoth with the Norman Duke?
Thus did'st thou break the word that thou hast given?

Harold.

Mother, thou must not in this hour be angered,
Across the sea to William will I go
And bring to thee the boy.

Edward.

Thou, Harold, thou?

Harold.

Yes, gracious Sire.

Edward.

Nay, Harold, go not thou.
That were to venture in the lion's den.

Harold.

Thou need'st but give me from thy hand a token,
That as a messenger from thee I come.

Edward.
To go thou art determined?

Harold.
Most determined.

Edward.
As far as these mine arms can reach thee, Harold,
I'll stretch them shieldingly above thy head.
The land thou goest to is full of dangers —
Yet dwelleth there an angel pure and bright
And I will place thee 'neath it's sheltering wings.

(he takes from his neck a chain on which a portrait is hung and gives it to Harold.)

Harold (gazes at the portrait).
What heavenly countenance is here depicted?

Edward.
It is Adéle's picture — t'is his daughter.

Gytha (taking the portrait from Harold).
Daughter of whom?

Edward.
Of William of the Normans.
Give him the picture; deep in this man's heart
Where wild ambition rages, is a spot,
Where fairest spring-time reigneth undisturbed
There dwells Adéle, his beloved child.
He gave me promise that who'eer should come
To him from me, protected by this picture,
Should as a trusted friend, to him be sacred. —

Harold.

Pray then dismiss me.

Edward.

         Go upon thy way —
And come again as joyous as thou goest.

(Edward L. Stigand exeunt C)

Ordgar

England is fatherless when thou dost leave us —
My gracious sir return to us right soon.

Harold.

Mix nought of sorrow in this day of joy,
Soon my good people soon I will return.

Gytha.

Go! I would speak now with my son alone.

(the citizens exeunt L. Gytha approaches Harold and gazes fix-edly at him.)

The Saxon stands upon the ocean shore,
Counteth each wave that from the south doth roll,
Seeketh each penant waving from the mast —
When will the longed for vessel come to sight?
When comes the hero back unto his people?

Harold.

What dark forebodings lie within thy words?
Give me the picture, it protects thy son.

Gytha.

But who will answer to me for his soul?

(folding him in her arms.)

Think of thy childless mother o my son!
Think of thy people left without a guide!
O bring me Godwin's son unchanged again.

72

Harold.

Mother beloved, what fears't thou?

Gytha.

Ask me not:
To name a danger is to call it forth.

Harold.

Yes truly when it lives but in our fancy.

(he looks smilingly at her.)

Ah mother is thine heart so poor in troubles
That it must needs beget yet more itself?
Before thou thinkest, I'll again be with thee,
And all thy anxious dreams shall be outdreamed.

(he places his arm round her neck and goes out slowly with her l. — as they leave the stage, the Curtain falls.)

Fnd of the second Act.

Act 3.

Scene 1.
(a thickly wooded forest landscape)

(Enter Odo. Randolf. Then Eustace of Boulogne. (from L.)
(all three are armed.)

Eustace.

The spot is chosen well: yon is the road
That leads to Rouen. (pointing L.)
                    And our watchers say
He is no longer far — here let us wait,
And he'll escape us not.

Odo.
                    He comes alone?

Eustace.

Without a soul; for those who came with him
The Earl of Ponthieu, (on whose territory
He put on shore), hath in their ships detained, —
Harold set forth upon his way alone.

Randolf.

And he shall no more see the town of Rouen
Than shall his followers.

74

Eustace.

We are resolved,
That he shall live no longer.

Randolf.

He shall lie
And rot amid these bushes. Death to him
Who drove us forth with mockery from England!

Odo.

Have ye inquired what Duke William holds
Of this your plan?

Eustace.

Fool were I, had I done so.
In such a matter questions are not asked.

Odo.

The Duke will sanction it?

Eustace.

By God in heaven,
How should he not? Is Harold, Edwards friend,
Then England is no longer for Duke William.
Dost understand?

Odo.

Down down then with the Saxon
Without delay!

Randolf (listening R.).

Still still, what noise is that?
I hear a rustling.

(goes hurriedly behind the scenes — R.)

Most accursed chance,
Princess Adéle nears us with her ladies.

Eustace (also looking R.)

Thou Odo art with Eleanor acquainted,
Take her aside and bid her in some manner
Lead the princess away from out the forest.
Meanwhile we will conceal us in the thicket.

(Eustace and Randolf disappear L. — Odo towards the back — R.)

(Enter **Adéle**. **Wulfnoth**, holding her hand. **Alice** (from R; they carry
short hunting spears in their hands, and seat themselves on mossy stones placed near
the front of the stage).

Adéle (to Alice).

Dost thou believe what Eleanor declares,
That love is nothing but a game for men?

Alice.

Ah nothing knoweth Eleanor of love,
It is not true.

Adéle.

             I too can scarce believe it,
Thou'rt surely in the right.

(to Wulfnoth)

             Art weary love?

Wulfnoth.

Not I.

Adéle.

Then come and be our little knight
And gather us a posy of wild roses
From yonder rose bush.

(Wulfnoth goes across the stage to a rosebush — L. — begins pleeching roses.)

             How this Saxon child
Has twined himself around my very heart.

Alice.

He has a gentle and endearing nature.

Adéle.

See his bright locks — lov'st thou their golden tint
As well as I?

Alice.

      I love a browner hue
Just such as thine.

Adéle.

         Ay, ay! thou honied flatterer
        (Wulfnoth brings roses.)
Now say for whom is this one?

Wulfnoth.

      For my mother.

Adéle.

Good — and the second? — How? Thou must consider?

Wulfnoth.

This is for thee and for my brother Harold.

Adéle (to Alice).

His second word is ever brother Harold.
One rose for two of us? well let me have it,
Lov'st thou us both alike?

Wulfnoth (caressing her).

      Yes quite alike.

(Enter **Eleanor** to the former from R.).

Eleanor.

Enough of resting, come princess Adéle,
I pray thee come or we shall miss the chase.

Adéle.

Enough of hunting — I'll no more to-day.

Eleanor.

Then let us homeward ride.

Adéle.

           Ah no not yet;
The breeze is soft, the birds so sweetly sing,
T'is pleasant resting on the mossy stones.

Eleanor.

Art thou so weary? or has lady Alice
Infected you with gentle dreaming fancies?

Adéle (to Alice).

Ah how this Eleanor must ever plague thee.

Alice.

Yes if she knew but how to rule her tongue
E'en as her horses —

Eleanor.

           But in earnest come.
All is not as it should be in this forest.
Ye know they say the thicket here is haunted
With evil spirits.

Adéle.
Do they say so Alice?

Alice.
I've heard it said good spirits here do dwell.

Eleanor.
Believe her not; the spirits are not good.
I pray thee — come!

Adéle.
Thou speakest as if truly
Thou'st seen a spirit?

Eleanor.
And — and, if it were so?

Adéle.
How Eleanor, thou art in very earnest?
What saw'st thou?

Eleanor.
That which I will tell thee later,
Come only now away from out the forest.

Adéle.
But are we not upon my father's grounds?
What saw'st thou?

Eleanor (whispering).
There are men within the wood,
They wait for some one   they are fully armed —
Up to their very teeth — in shining steel.

Adéle (Springing to her feet).

Can they be robbers?

Eleanor.

        Robbers they are not;
For they are barons of thy father's court;
Odo is one of them, the second Eustace.
And yet a third whose face I did not know.

Adéle.

Eustace and Odo? Late arived from England?
Laying in wait? For whom?

Eleanor.

       I cannot tell thee,
But did I ever read in human eyes
A foul and bloody purpose clearly written,
Is it in these. My sweetest Mistress come,
Else do I fear that we may here behold
Some sight most horrible.

Adèle.

       Away, away.

(At the same moment that she turns to go out R, — Wulfnoth runs across the stage to L. and points behind the scenes).

Wulfnoth.

My brother Harold!

(exit L.)

Adéle.

       Jesus, holy Saviour!
(falling back on the stone.)
Now know I whom their bloody purpose threatens!

Eleanor.

Come come away — come hence —

(a shrill whistle is heard behind the scenes.)

Adéle (springs up).

Hark! heard ye that?
What should I do? What not do? Help me heaven!

(She covers her eyes despairingly with her hands.)

A stranger — t'is against all modest custom —
Bah! modest custom! T'is a human being!

(She rushes hastily behind the scenes L. and calls.)

Dismount I pray thee sir — dismount this moment —
Make fast thy horse's reins — and come — come hither —

(she turns to Alice and Eleanor.)

Now dearest maidens — shew me that ye love me —
Mount suift your horses — hasten to my father —
There's none will hinder ye, they will not dare —
Say to my father that his child much needs him!

Eleanor.

Mistress, we fly.

Alice.

Dear lady, courage — courage!

(Both hasten out R.)

Adéle (going a few steps further behind the scenes).

Thy hand — I pray thee — come o come I pray —

(Enter **Harold** led by Adéle) **Wulfnoth** holding his other hand from L.).

Adéle.

I fear me much that thou must deem me bold —
But here — in Normandy — it is our custom. —

(she lets his hand fall.)

Harold (gazing wonderingly at her).

(aside) It is the very picture that he gave me --
Beauteous and fair as is the heaven above us.
(aloud) Do I not err, thou art Duke William's daughter!
Princess Adéle?

Wulfnoth (throwing his arms round her).

Yes, it is Adéle!

Adéle.

Denying serves me not since he betrays me.

Harold.

Then grant me sweet fulfilment of my duty
And let me thank my kind, protecting angel.
Know'st thou the talisman that decks my breast?
(he kisses her hand and shews her the portrait attached to the chain round her neck.)

Adéle.

My portrait —

Harold.

Trusted to me by king Edward,
That it secure unto me kind reception

Adéle.

Thou comest hither — hath not fear detained thee?

Harold.

Ah no, I fear not.

Adéle.

Thou! — Thou dost not fear?

Harold.

Duty hath led me hither.

(a second shrill whistle is heard behind the scenes.)

What was that?

I heard it once before —

Adéle (calling loudly).

Swift swift — thy hand!

Harold (turning round).

What men are these approaching.

(Eustace, Odo and Randolf appear in the background in wild agitation, their faces concealed. Harold goes toward the back of the stage.)

Adéle

(holding him back with invo-luntary force.)

Stay! o stay!

Remain! I pray thee!

(Harold remains standing in astonishment — Adéle calls to the back of the stage.)

Sirs, the chase is ended,

Ye can return — I need no more your service —

(Eustace, Randolf and Odo disappear L.)

Harold.

The chase? I'st custom here to hunt with swords
And helmet-covered heads?

Adéle.

Ah — went they — hence? —

What was't thou saidest — what? —

Harold.

Princess Adéle —

What shall I think of this? By God in heaven —

Adéle (stammering faintly).

A chase — t'was but a chase — ah — as thou see'st —
We have most wondrous customs in our country.

*(Enter **Duke William. The Seneschal. Alice. Eleanor** from L., to the former).*

Adéle.

He comes — my father — ah — now all is well.

(she falls back fainting, Harold catches her in his arms.)

Alice *(hastening up to her).*

O my beloved mistress what has chanced?

(Alice and Eleanor take Adéle from Harold and lead her slowly to one of the mossy stones where she gradually recovers herself.)

William.

My child! pale pale as death and here — a stranger —
(to Harold) Who art thou?

Harold *(bending low before William).*

Harold, gracious Sir, from England.

William.

Harold, the son of Godwin?

Harold.

With this token,
From Edward king of England sent to thee.

(he takes the chain from his neck and gives it to William.)
(pause.)
(William looks in silence first at Harold, then at Adéle.)

William.

It sheweth trust to judge a fellow-being
As t'were one's self — thou, Harold trustest me —
Henceforth I know thee. — We have once been foes,
Say Harold, wilt thou try to be my friend?

ACT 3.

Harold.
I will Duke William from my very heart.
(he bends on one knee before William.)

William
(replaces the chain round his neck).
Thus with this chain the second time I bind thee;
Arise and be most welcome to my court.

Transformation.

Scene 2.

A park at Rouen. (In the foreground R. a grassy mound — Attendants and Pages enter from R. carying Weapons Dishes, Cushions Ornaments and all kinds of preparations for a great Festival — thy cross over toward the back of the stage — L.)

(Enter First and Second Attendant (from R.)

First Attendant.
Which of the horses does duke Harold ride
To-day at the great tourney?

Second Attendant.
        Well, I heard
He'll ride the Duke's own grey.

First Attendant.
        His special favourite?

Second Attendant.
He'll have it so.

First Attendant.

Then let us make a bet.
I bet upon Montgomery.

Second Attendant.

I too.

First Attendant.

We cannot bet upon the selfsame horse,
T'was I spoke first.

Second Attendant.

That's all the same to me,
I still will bet upon Montgomery.

First Attendant.

Then I'll bet on the Saxon.

Second Attendant.

As thou willst.

First Attendant.

He'll have Montgomery down upon the ground
As though he were a feather!

Second Attendant.

Say't again,
And I will knock thy teeth into thy throat.

(exeunt both.)

(Enter **Harold. The Seneschal** from R.)

Seneschal.

See with what eagerness they all bestir them.
Ah yes a tourney is the fairest feast
Of all in this our merry Normandy.
But thee it pleases not.

Harold.

Thou dost me wrong,
Who doth not feel his heart more swiftly beat
At sight of a festivity so knightly?

Seneschal.

And yet thou art resolved so soon to leave us?
Before the tourney?

Harold.

Ay I must from hence —
Thou hast preferred my boon unto the duke?
He'll give to me the child?

Seneschal.

And thou could'st doubt it?

Harold.

He gave thee no refusal? Did not waver?

Seneschal.

Thou seem'st to wonder! Yet he was agreed.

Harold (aside).

Then am I free. —
(A Page crosses the stage, carrying a cushion, upon which lire a veil embroidered
in gold.)

Seneschal (stopping the Page).

See here this gauzy veil,
It is the second prize our umpire places
Upon the helmet of the second victor.

Harold.

The second prize — and what then is the first?

Seneschal.

That is a wreath of gold; our lady umpire
Herself doth place it on the victor's brow:
Then pressing it upon his locks, she bendeth
To gentle kiss.

Harold.

A kiss the victor's prize?

Seneschal.

An ancient custom doth permit this freedom.

Harold.

Who is the umpire?

Seneschal.

T'is Duke William's daughter. —

Harold.

Princess Adéle!?

Seneschal.

Ay! but see, the Duke. —

(Enter **William** (from R. to the former).

William.

The seneschal doth bring unwelcome tidings
Thou wilt from hence?

Harold.

My duty calls me, Duke.

William.

Meseems it hath but little pleased thee with us,
Since thou so hastenest?

Harold.

Prithee think not thus,
Perchance because it pleased me all too well,
Must I from hence.

William.

Ah cold and earnest Saxon —
So richly gifted by the hand of nature
Wiuh keenest sense and power of enjoyment,
Yet thus from joy to shrink? Believe me, Harold
It grieves me sorely that thou goest hence.

Harold.

Ah Duke — no more.

William (significantly).

Yet Harold — let me speak:
If to the stern true nature of the Saxon
The Norman's fiery spirit were united,
A people would be founded that on earth,
Could find no equal.

Harold.

Ay but such alliance
Doth signify: „One rules, the other-serves".

William.

But how if both of them should serve one master
To whom both well were known and rightly valued.

Harold.

Give me my brother pray thee gracious sir,
That to his mother I may safely bring him?

William.

The boy is at thy service when thou wilt,
Ah see, Adéle comes and brings him hither.

(Enter **Adéle** (festively attired) from R. She leads **Wulfnoth** by the hand)

William (to Adéle).

Come hither daughter, our well-honoured guest
Obedient to the call of kin and country,
At once will leave us to set forth for England.
(to Harold)
Your pardon that a moment I withdraw,
Some questions of the tourney need my presence.
(exeunt William and Seneschal — R.)

Adéle.

So thou wilt leave me cruel little Wulfnoth?
Soon will Adéle be by thee forgotten;
Is't not so?

Wulfnoth (embracing her tenderly).

Never! —

Adéle.

Thou wilt not forget me?
Wilt sometimes think of me?

Wulfnoth.

I pray thee come,
Come with me to my mother?

90

Adéle.

Gentle prattler!

Harold.

For all that thou hast done for this young child
Accept thy servant's warm and heartfelt thanks.

Adéle.

It shameth me that for such easy service
An earnest man should give such earnest thanks.

Harold.

If thou dost care not to receive my thanks,
Think that the mother of this child doth speak
Through me to thee to thank thee for thy kindness.

Adéle.

Ah yes — his mother who is thine as well —
O hard, most hard must it have been for her,
To know both children here amid their foes?

Harold.

Ay, for she knew not the protecting spirit
That gently guarded o'er her absent sons.
Thou deemest light what for the child thou'st done;
Ah feel, how from this azure vault of heaven
Life streameth down and fills our souls with bliss;
Is that too light that thou hast done for him .
Who lived to-day no more wer't not for thee?

Adéle.

Ah think no more upon that hour I pray thee.

Harold.

No more I'll speak of it, but in my heart
Remembrance weds that hour with thy fair image
For ever — ever - gentlest mistress say
Dost rue the kindness thou to me hast granted?

Adéle.

Nay — in good truth — and thou to-day dost leave us?

Harold.

It must be so.

Adéle.

      Then if — it truly must be —
Confide the child once more unto my charge
That for the journey I prepare him well.

Harold.

Princess, we now must part. — It seemeth wondrous —

Adéle.

What seemeth wondrous?

Harold.

      That I cannot think
That ever in my life there was a time
When thee I knew not. — Ah princess Adéle,
The word of pain „farewell" must now be spoken,
Adéle, my protectress — fare thee well!

(exit L.)

Adéle

(stands for a few moments lost in deep thought, then turns to Wulfnoth).

A marvel t'is — the likeness to his brother!

(she kneels down before the boy, takes his head between her hands and gazes
at him attentively.)

92

Wulfnoth.

What doest thou Adéle?

Adéle.
Still, sweet love.
The brow — like his. — The mouth almost, not quite,
Not yet so firm — the eyes the very same!
O, wondrous well must God have loved these beings
When he created them: for in their eyes
He laid a fragment of his own blue heavens.
(she kisses the child's eyes.)
Thus drink I at the source of purest light.
Lov'st thou thy brother Harold?

Wulfnoth.
Dearly!

Adéle.
Child —
(kisses him)
Give this to him again —

Wulfnoth.
To whom?

Adèle.
Come — come!
(she rises from her knees and goes quickly out with Wulfnoth.)
(Harold has returned unperceived during the last few words.)

Harold
(advancing to the front of the stage).

And were it at the peril of my soul,
No more of parting — nought shall now divide us,
Here is the spot to me for ever blest!
„Give this to him again" — entrancing tone,

Pierce to my heart and in it's inmost depths
Stifle the dull, sepulchral voice of conscience.
This is the spot on which her gentle knee
Hath left it's impress on the happy soil,
Where to the lips of the unconscious child
Her lips the message of her heart confided —
O all the ground around this spot is holy
Through the pure sacrifice of her sweet love.

(Enter **William. Seneschal** (from R.)

Harold.

I fear me Duke, thou'lt chide me for my whims;
With thy permission I'll await the tourney.
The tourney over, I would still abide,
And so stay on until thou bid'st me go.

William.

Harold, by God that day thou ne'er shalt see!
And once again I bid thee hearty welcome:
Ho Seneschal come quickly and attend him:
With mine own weapons gird him for the fight.
Then on to victory.

Harold.

          I would t'were mine!
Come God of victory come, and bless my weapons!
(exeunt Harold and Seneschal — R.)

William (alone).

O fate I ask thee make this man my friend!
For Harold can'st thou love duke William's daughter,
Why not love William's mightly plan as well,
And do him therein great and serious service?

.

94

(Enter **Robert of Jumièges**. Wilfried (from L.)

W i l l i a m (hastening to Robert).

Good that thou comest. — Thinkest thou that Harold
Doth know that I am heir unto king Edward.

R o b e r t.

I'll stake my life as pledge, he knows it not;
Thou may'st be certain nought hath Edward told him.
(flourish of trumpets behind the scenes.)

W i l l i a m.

Heard'st thou?

R o b e r t.
I heard indeed but know not what?

W i l l i a m.

Yonder with all his strength doth Harold strive
To win a kiss from off my daughter's lips.

R o b e r t.

What sayest thou?

W i l l i a m.

Thou know'st the Saxon, Bishop —
I know thou lov'st him not, I love him well,
My heart is drawn most strongly to this man —
Myself doth scarce know why. — How if I ask him
What t'was that Edward promised me.

R o b e r t.
And then?

William.

Why then — the prize for which his heart so longeth,
My child Adéle will I give to him
He in return shall give me England's crown —
Bishop — should he be ready?

Robert.

Never! never!

William.

Ha, curse and death!

Robert.

If thou would'st have me flatter,
I could say yes; because I am thy friend
I say what well I know: t'is past conceiving.

William.

Thou scatterest my hopes unto the ground
With this one word.

Robert.

Nay nought is lost Duke William,
If thou dost ask the question with more caution!
Is it thy purpose that to that he help thee,
Which Edward promised — speak in general terms,
But say thou nought anent the crown of England.

William.

A sapient counsel; and if he should ask
What t'was that Edward promised?

Robert.

Let him think
That it concerned alone the promised fiefdom
Of Edward's lands that lie in Normandy
Of this he heard from Edward.

William.
Could I do this?

Robert.
If thou art wise. First give to him thy daughter,
And let his bosom's rigid chastity . ...
Melt 'neath the sunny charms of thy Adéle,
Till lulled within the gentle arms of habit
And clinging to thee with a son's affection,
All thou can'st tell him: then from thee he'll learn
What t'was he promised thee with holy oath.

William.
An oath? what oath?

Robert.
Ah yes! I had forgotten —
Methinks t'were safer if thou now demandest
That he should swear, in presence of thy Barons,
With solemn oath to help thee unto all
That Edward promised thee. — And should it chance
That later he repenteth of his promise,
His oath still bindeth him by life and death.

William.
Nay — that mispleases me.

Robert.
Bethink thee duke,
T'is but a caution. When he learneth all,
Repentance will but me'lt away in love.

William.
But I shall stand with blush of shame before him
And that I can not.

7

Robert.

One thing else remains:
Living he dare no more return to England.

William.

I gave my word; the picture that he brought me
Is pledge of safety to him.

Robert.

If it be so? —
Then I advise — renounce the crown of England.

William.

To conquer him with cunning — to play out
My child against him e'en like cheating dice
Upon the dice board — T'is byeond belief
He help me to the crown?

Robert.

Past all believing.
(pause.)

William.

Then it must be. — O England that I buy thee
With gold so false!

Robert.

I will myself be present
When Harold sweareth; for am I the witness,
The oath is sanctioned by the holy church.

William.

Thou shalt be present — ah, whom have we here?
(percieving Wilfried.)
Hath not thy deacon overheard our words?

Robert.

That matters nothing for his soul exists
Alone in mine.

William.

T'is good — farewell till later
(exit R.)

Robert (to Wilfried).

Thou heardest all that we together spoke?

Wilfried.

I heard it all.

Robert.

Then know it is thy duty
Ne'er to repeat it unto other ears.

Wilfried.

Is this the will of God?

Robert

Thou darest doubt it
When t'is thy bishop who himself doth say so.

Wilfried.

From me shall no one hear it.

Robert.

Go before me.

(Wilfried goes out L. As Robert is leaving the stage **Adéle** appears hurriedly
from R.).

Robert.

The tourney is already ended?

Adéle.

No!

But soon — almost!

Robert.
　　　Thou waitest not the end?

Adéle.

Help me to pray my father —

Robert.
　　　　　And for what?

A déle (throwing herself down upon the grassy mound).
My God, my God! O how will all this end!

(Enter **William** (from R.).
Adéle here, forgetful of her duty?

Robert.
Forgetful of her duty?

William.
　　　From the tourney,
The which as umpire doth demand her presence,
She stole away.

A déle (embracing him passionately).
　　　Ah let me not be umpire!

William.
Who else but thou? Thou wilt not keep the custom?

Adéle.
Ah let me break the custom of a game
Before I — ah —

Robert.

What aileth thee my daughter?

Adéle.

Before I break all customs good and holy.
(She conceals her face on her father's breast: William and Robert exchange
significant glances.)

Robert.

My Duke, I beg permission to retire.
(William bows assent. Exit Robert L.)

William.

Adéle say what hast thou?

Adéle.

Father hearken:
I cannot give to him the victor's prize!

William.

To Harold?

Adéle.

E'en to Harold.
(trembling.)
O my God!

William.

But I will have it so.

Adéle.
Ah no!

William.

Thy reason?

Adéle.

Why? Why? Ah did my mother still but live,

(she looks earnestly into his face shaking her head,)

And thou — so wise, so great, that thou can'st ask me?

William.

Dost thou so hate him?

Adéle.

Hate him! Such a man!

William.

Dost thou so love him?

Adéle.

Father ask no more!

William.

He loveth thee?

Adéle.

Ah had he never come!

William.

Thou foolish child — and if I were to tell thee,
Your mutual love doth much rejoice my heart?

Adéle.

O, can it be? And it is no delusion?
Thou William, Duke of Normandy and he,
The son of thy worst foe? For so I thought it.

William.

So t'is but through thy love he is my friend.

102

Adéle.

O happy, happy dream! But ah, my father,
Thou dost not wantonly deceive thy child?
Thou speak'st in earnest?

William.

        Deepest earnest, daughter.

Adéle.

And I may dare to call myself so blest!

William.

That mayest thou.

Adéle.

        His bright and glorious image
Dare dwell like living fire within my heart?
(Trompets from R.)

William.

Listen —· the trumpets warn us he approaches.
The pages bear the wreath — thou know'st thy duty.

(Enter from R.: pages, one of whom carries a wreath of gold upon a purple cushion: the Seneschal and a mumber of barons enter, then Harold, followed by the Duke's retinue. The page approaches Adéle: she takes the wreath from the cushion — advances to the front, where she remains standing with down cast eyes.)

Seneschal.

My gracious duke, —- we hither bring the victor.
A hero knight, of heroes the most knightly.

William

(approaches Harold, and leads him by the hand to Adéle).

My noble guest the umpire stands before thee.
Demand of her the well deserved reward.

Harold (standing before Adéle).

Nay not deserved, thy grace alone doth grant
Such high reward: sweet lady of thy grace
Raise thy soft eyelids — give to me the prize.

Adéle.

And shall my hand adorn the victor's brow,
Must I beseech thee: bend thy lofty head.

Harold (bending on one knee before her).

Bend I now low enough?

Adéle.

        Thou dost beshame me.

(she places the wreath upon his head.)

Even as with thy golden locks I wed
This golden wreath — may brightest fame and honour
Be ever wedded to the victor Harold.

Harold.

Ah — thou dost wed me unto mighty things!
Yet sweeter things than these I fair would wed.

Adéle.

I pray thee rise Duke Harold.

Harold.

Let me kneel,
Until thou grantest me the whole reward

(Adéle glances at her father William and the barons retire slowly to the back
of the stage and exeunt R.)

O tremble not.

Adéle.

Thou knowest?

Harold.

Yes, I know.

Adéle.

(gazes into his face, then placing her hands on his shoulders, bends towards him.)

Ah — Harold — Harold —

(she kisses him.)

Harold.

Ecstacy of bliss!

(he folds her in his arms and presses a kiss upon her lips.)

„Give this to him again“, I thus restore it.

Adéle (trembling).

Ah I am lost!

Harold (springing up and supporting her).

Say rather thou art found
By one who knows he finds a priceless treasure!

(he leads her to the grassy mound and seats himself beside her.)

Harold.

Sweet love — o let me now no longer rest
Upon the threshold of unmeasured bliss;
With all my soul I love thee fair Adéle.

Adéle.

Can this be truth?

Harold.
　　Thou doubtest?

Adéle.
　　　　No, ah no!
Dost thou remember that when first I saw thee
An earnest man I called thee?

Harold.
　　　　　I remember.

Adéle.

An earnest man — it seems a simple word —
Yet did'st thou know the import that it bears
Within my heart, then truly would'st thou say,
No greater praise can woman's lips bestow.

Harold.
And thou dost praise me thus?

Adéle.
　　　　It means a man
Who ne'er in lightness or in idle pastime
Could speak the precious words thou speak'st to me.

Harold.
May God forlid? Those words were solemn earnest.

Adéle.
Then dare I now conceal from thee no more,
That when for the first time thy glance I met,
It seemed a source so pure and undefiled,
That one it's very deepest ground might fathom.

106

Harold.

Angel of purity such thought was thine?

Adéle.

Harold beloved — ah know'st thou how I love thee?
<small>(they embrace.)</small>

Harold.

Firm to eternity our bond shall prove ――
This day I'll pray thy father for his child -

Adéle.

Hear dear one, hear from me the happy tidings,
My father knoweth all.

Harold.

   Thy father knoweth?

Adéle.

He knoweth and rejoiceth in our love.

Harold.

And he doth sanction it?

Adéle.

   He'd be thy friend.

Harold <small>(rising).</small>

Ah now I know —

Adéle.

   What knowest thou dear love?

Harold,
That thou'rt in truth a spirit fair of light
Fore which all doubt must flee. —
(looking)
Behold thy father

Adéle (springing up).
Ah then away!

Harold (retaining her in his embrace).
Nay stay — ah stay Adéle —
That I may gaze once more upon thy face.
O morning light of hope in these fair eyes!
Now will I speak with him.

Adéle.
Ah Harold — Harold!
(exit L.)

(Enter William (from R.).

Harold.

William thou know'st that when thou cam'st to England,
No name so hateful unto me did sound
As did thine own: so t'was, but that is changed
Since I have learnt to know thy name's great worth.
Permit me honoured Duke with thee to speak
As it befits one true man to another:
I love thy child.
William.
Adéle?

Harold.
Even so!
And ask thee for her hand.

108

William.

Alas t'is bitter
That unto thee this boon I must refuse.

Harold.

How? thou refusest me?

William.

By God not I!
Were I a noble knight with scanty lands
And thou e'en such as I and cam'st to woo,
By God I'd pluck away this gentle flower
My child Adéle, out my bleeding heart
To plant it in the garden of thy life. —
For well I love thee Harold! — Yet we great ones
Are but the fettered slaves of circumstance!
The rest thou knowest; let me now be silent.

Harold.

T'is for the sake then of thy Norman people
That thou refusest me?

William.

For this alone,
Yet t'is enough; they see in thee my foe,
And ne'er would they forgive me such an union.

Harold.

To let me prove in presence of thy people
That I no longer am thine enemy:
Ask what thou will'st for thy Adéle's hand.

William (after a moment's pause).

Thou know'st what t'was that led me into England,
And know'st the promise that king Edward gave me?

Harold.

He said that he had pledged to thee his word.
Anent an heritage in Normandy —
This promise of the king it is thou meanest?
(pause.)

William.

Yes, yes the heritage — e'en so, now say
That thou wilt help me that I shall attain
All that which Edward, England's king did promise. —
(he stretches out his hand.)
It seems too much? — thou doubtest?

Harold.

It shall be so —

I will not weigh with usurer's deep caution
The gift that in return to thee I owe,
For thy most precious, priceless, royal present —
(giving his hand.)
Harold will help thee to attain to all
That Edward, England's king to thee did promise.

William.

With thousand fibres twine around my heart.
(they embrace.)

William.

Forgive my troubling thee with tedious form.
(pointing R.)
I see the barons of my court approaching,
With thou now in their presence take an oath,
Repeating that which thou to me hast promised?
Thou know'st t'is but a form.

110

Harold.

And I am ready
To swear to that which I to thee have promised.

(Enter **Seneschal, Montgomery** end **other norman Barons** from R.
to the former.   **pages** bearing tankards and goblets come from L.).

William.

Ho! wine and goblets! We will drink thee welcome;
Harold I pray of thee to test this wine.
(The pages pour wine into the goblets which they offer around.)

Harold.

The wine is good? In what bright glowing chamber
Of her vast workshop breweth mother earth
Such draught as this?

William.

I'm glad that it doth please thee.
Blood of the Norman is the name it bears.

Harold.

Thus floweth Norman blood into my veins.

Seneschal.

My gracious Duke methinks t'is fitting place. —
But lately from a minstrel well approved
I learnt a song that's new —
(to William)

Thou dost permit --

William.

Ay Seneschal, come season wine with song.

111

Seneschal (advancing to the foreground sings).

Gaze on the earth so beauteous and bright,
The mountains, the valleys, so fair to the sight;
Dost know what enticing her glance to thee speaks?
„The blossom's for him who the blossom breaks."
To the bold and the daring, the brave and the strong
The earth will obey and the world will belong!
So whether a Saxon or Norman he be,
I'll prize the brave champion, the bold and the free!

Harold (drinks)

That is a song such as I love to hear,
It makes the silent heart within us speak!

Seneschal.

Gaze on the flowers so beauteous and bright,
The maidens so lovely, so fair to the sight!
Dost know what so shyly their glance to thee speaks?
The blossom's for him who the blossom breaks.
With her who hath bound us with love's gentle chains
Our heart in sweet bondage for ever remains. —
Then whether a Saxon or Norman he be,
I'll prize the brave champion, the bold and the free!

Montgomery.

Then Saxon or Norman, which'eer it may be
We'll drink to the brave, to the bold and the free!
(All let their glasses clink together.)

William (raising his goblet.
I drink to Harold to my future son!

Seneschal.

To whom?

Montgomery.
How so?

William.
No longer are we foes:
I give to him my daughter, my Adéle,
And he doth help to make me Edward's heir.

Seneschal.
This he will do?

Montgomery.
T'is true?

William.
To prove it is so,
Before ye all he'll take a solemn oath.
Speak I the truth, Duke Harold?

Harold.
As thou knowest.

Seneschal (looking L.)
Ah that is well; the Bishop cometh hither.

(Enter **Robert, Wilfried** (from L. Wilfried carries a Crucifix).

Harold (starts back at the sight of Robert.)

Robert.
Thou know'st the oath thou art about to take?

Harold.
Am I a child? I pray thee to the purpose.

Robert.

Place now thy hands upon this cruciffx.
(Wilfried kneels down and holds the crucifix aloft.)
Say, will'st thou help Duke William of the Normans
Unto the heritage that Edward promised?

Harold (aside).

The heritage? He means the Norman lands.
Yes yes — I recollect — so said king Edward —
(he lays both his hands on the crucifix.)
To help the Norman William to attain
Unto the heritage that Edward promised
I hereby swear.
(lets his hands fall.)
         Therewith is this completed.

William.

Now is Adéle, soul and body thine.
(hastens out L.)

Robert.

Thou know'st thou'st sworn upon the holy cross.

Harold.

What I have done I know. An oath's an oath.

Seneschal.

For all the suffering that till now thou'st born,
He will as king right royally repay thee.

Robert. (excitedlly).

Peace Seneschal!

Harold.

         What is there to conceal?
As king? whom mean ye?

Eustace (suddenly entering from R.).

William, king of England.

Harold

Count of Boulogne? By Jesus holy cross —
King Edward promised —

Eustace.

That upon his death,
William the Norman should be king of England.

Harold.

By God's death — no!

Eustace and the Barons.

By God's great glory, yes!

Harold (casts himself in wild despair upon the ground).

Earth burst asunder! Light of day be darkened!
Betrayed! betrayed in all that is most holy!

Seneschal.

Be calm my gracious Sir.

Harold.

And I have sworn
Upon the holy crucifix! Hence hence, away!
Let none approach me -- hence, away, away!
(he springs to his feet and staggers out.)
(great agitation amongst the Normans.)

Eustace.

This is no fitting time to stand and gaze!
Montgomery belay with careful watchers
Each outlet from the palace and the garden.
Your death if he escape.

A Norman.

No fear of that!

(exit R.)

And now unto the Duke — ah hither comes he.

(Enter **William** to the former from L.

Eustace (going towards him).

My gracious Duke our well-formed plan has failed.
Scarce had he heard the meaning of his oath —

William.

Damnation to ye all, if this has chanced!
From whom then did he hear it?

Eustace.

Duke, from me.

William.

A curse upon thy all too ready zeal.

(to Robert)

And thou wer't present and did'st nought prevent it?

Robert.

Too suddenly it came to intervene.

Eustace.

It grieves me that my zeal doth so misplease thee,
Yet now bethink thee what t'were best to do.
His oath repenting, should he now escape thee,
He'll flee from, even as he flees from thee.

William.

Bishop — he rues it?

Robert.

                    With a fierce repentance
With wildest ravings forth from us he rushed
And fled into the park.

Eustace.

                    We have him safe:
Palace and garden were at once surrounded,
Harold is in thy hands.
                    (pause.)

William (fiercely).

                    Then learn thou Saxon,
The hand that unto thee so freely gave
Like to the hand of God holds life and death!
Thou Seneschal go hasten to my daughter
Take the child Wulfnoth quickly from her keeping
And bring him to a place of strict confinement.

Seneschal.

It shall be done my Duke.
                    (exit L.)

William.

                    To thee count Eustace
I trust the rest.

Eustace.

                    And safely thou may'st trust me
By God I'll see that he be guarded well!
(William, Robert and Wilfried exeunt L. Eustace and the Barons R.)

(After a short pause, **Harold** enters from R. and casts himself upon the grassy mound.)

Harold.

Close guarded is each outlet from the garden —
The traitor in the might of the betrayer —

(it begins to grow dank.)

Hide me o night, concealer dark of crime.
Melt all my thoughts into a misty nothing,
Let nought be clear — for clearness bringeth death.

(Enter **Adéle** from R.).

Harold.

Who cometh hither? Ah, that step I know!

(gazing around.)

The daughter of the Norman.

Adéle (stops terrified).

Harold, thou?

Harold (going up to her and gazing steadfastly at her)

Thou maiden, on whose visage God in heaven
Printed the likeness of his purest angels,
Give me an answer to this single question:
Hast thou deceived me or wert thou deceived?

Adéle.

What have I done to thee, that thou should'st ask it?

Harold.

Ah no, these lips are innocent of lying.
He spared not e'en his own beloved child?
Unhappy noe.

Adéle.

Say Harold what has chanced?

Harold.

No fitting time is this for words, Adéle,
My path with threntening danger is surrounded.

Adéle.

What danger?

Harold.

Danger for my soul and body,
Hence must I flee.

Adéle.

But whither and from whom?

Harold.

That thou must ask of others not of me!
For when that name unto thine ear be told,
T'will fall like early frost in night of spring,
To poison all the faith of thy young soul.

Adèle.

Thou speak'st in cruel riddles.

Harold.

Come then hearken:
I must from hence; yet ev'ry garden entrance
Is guarded with the sword to bar my passage,
And ev'ry palace door is firmly closed.
Know'st thou a way of outlet, haste to shew it.

Adéle.

Come go with me, from out my chamber opens
A secret passage leading to the meadows:
I'll shew it thee —

Harold.

          Yet one thing more Adéle:
Thou hast my brother Wulfnoth in thy keeping;
Bring me the child.

Adéle.

'   Ah listen what has chanced;
This moment as I hither came to seek thee
The child was torn from me.

Harold.

          Ah death and hell!
Then must I flee alone. — Beloved Adéle,
I trust my brother to thy gentle keeping,
Protect and cherish the forsaken child.

Adéle.

Harold when comest thou again to seek him?

Harold.

Adéle, when?

Adéle.

       When see I thee once more?

Harold.

We meet the last, last time in life, to-day.

Adéle (despairingly).

O death most terrible! My heart will break!
(she clings to him wildly.)
Ah Harold, leave me not!

Harold.

Alas it must be.

Adéle

Where go'st thou?

Harold.
Far from hence.

Adéle.
Across — the sea?

Harold.

Across the sea!

Adéle.
Ah woe unto our love!
T'will sink and perish 'neath the deep cold waves.

Harold.
No — for t'will live in our immortal souls.
Sweet angel hold mine image in thine heart
As one doth hold the image of the lost,
Their faults in tender mercy all forgotten.
And should'st thou later hear thy loved one named
With curses and accused of bitterest crimes,
Then think: not of that Harold do they speak
Whom thou hast known: For he, in that same hour
When last he pressed a kiss upon those lips
That once had been his heaven, sank down and perished
Pure, in the deadly depths of the pure ocean.
Dream of my happy youth — farewell — farewell. —

(They cling to each other in a passionate embrace.)

The Curtain falls.

———

End of the third Act.

121

Act 4.

Scene 1.

(A hall in the palace at London. Doors and windows R. and L. In the background a row of columns the spaces between them filled up with curtains.)

(**King Edward** sits cowering in an arm chair, his eyes closed. **Edwin** and **Stigand** stand beside him.)

(Enter **Morcar** to the former.)

Morcar.

Yes it is true — the tidings are confirmed
That whispered low from mouth were born.
He has returned. In a small fishing vessel,
Without companions, in the gloom of night,
Surrounded by the terrors of the darkness
That had effaced the torchlight of the stars,
He, batt'ling 'gainst the wildly surging billows
Landed at early morn this day at Dover.

Edwin.

A fishing boat? At night? It is a fable?

Morcar.

No no, t'is truth. He has been seen by many
As in the first grey light of early morning
He sprang on shore all torn by waves and wind,
As were he being, born of night and ocean.

122

Edward (speaking with his eyes still closed).
Who is the being that your words surround
With such deep mysteries?

Edwin.

T'is Harold, sire.

Edward (arousing from his lethargy).
Has Harold come again from Normandy!

Morcar.
T'is he of whom I speak my gracious Sire —
Without a moment's greeting for his mother
And without resting his exhausted frame,
Seizing the swiftest charger from his stable,
He vaulted in the saddle — so t'was told me —
His spurs so driven in the horse's flanks,
That like an arrow flying from the bow
The fiery steed sprang forth beneath it's rider.

Stigand.
Whom was it that he sought with such wild speed?

Morcar.
To Winchester he rode, where through an error
He thought to find king Edward.

Edward.

Ha! I knew it,
It was to me he rode — too tardy death
Why suffer'st thou this day to overtake thee?

Stigand.
What fearst thou' Sire?

Edward.

Should'st thou ever hear
Of one complaining death had come too soon,
Reproach him for his folly, for I tell thee
Far better die too early than too late!

(be partly rises from his chair and remains motionless his eyes fixed on some
object in the background.)

Ha! what comes there — see — see! —

(Harold (has drawn back the curtain and appears in the background. He is pale
and his glance is wild; his head is uncovered, his long fair hair falls dishevelled
about him, his mantle is torn).

Stigand.

By God, t'is Harold.

Morcar.

And yet another — is it thou my nephew?

Harold.

Command these men to leave us, king of England!

(Edward gazes at him speechless).

Edwin.

Are we not good enough to hear thy tidings?

Harold (furiously).

Bid these men go —

Morcar.

We leave thee for the present.

(exeunt Edwin, Morcar, Stigand R.)
(Harold fastens the door upon them.)

124

Edward.

What work of deadly import dost thou purpose?
Harold — I am a weak and aged man.

Harold.

Would God that thou had'st ever been ought else.

Edward.

There is a tone within thy voice that's strange —
And in thy countenance a changed expression —
Why dost thou glare so with thy burning eyes?

Harold.

That they may read into thine inmost soul —
Edward thou son of Ethelred the Saxon,
I have a question I must put to thee:
Upon that day when William to thee came,
What was't thou promised him? Three days and nights
I grappled fieercely breast to breast with death
That I might ask this of thee — speak, give answer!

Edward.

Death knocketh at the portal of my life —
Ask not what t'was I promised, ask it not!

Harold.

Was it — and by the saviour's cross I ask thee —
Was it the truth the Norman William spoke,
That on thy death thou unto him had'st promised
The crown of England?

Edward.
      He himself hath said it?

Harold.

Is this the truth, o evil councilled king?

Edward.

And were it so — be merciful my son!

Harold.

Yes, yes thy son, in guilt we are related!

(Edward sinks back exhausted.)

Nay — sink not back, thou yet must live awhile;
The crime thou hast committed is my death;
With hellish plotting William did persuade me
That I should swear with solemn, holy oath
To help him to attain to all thou'st promised!

Edward.

Would God t'were not so! O unblessed Harold;
Had I but told thee all upon that day
Thou wentest forth from hence to Normandy —
Had I, ah had I — wretched summing up
Of life that's ended — cruel, cruel William!
And must he then be king of England?

Harold.

No!

Edward.

Play not with hope! Who dare prevent it?

Harold.

Harold!

Edward.

Thou who hast sworn? O daring one what wilt thou?

126

Harold.

The trait'rous oath that binds me will I break!
Ne'er will I give this Anglosaxou land
Into the greedy clutches of the Norman!

Edward.

This is thine earnest, Harold?

Harold.

By mine oath!
Yet no   ah, no I never more may swear!
O most immeasurable grief and shame!
Harold the son of Godwin, perjured! perjured!

(he prostrates himself on the earth.)

Here at thy feet I lie — almighty God,
Maker of human beings and their frailties,
Here freely do I forfeit and renounce
All that has once adorned my noble manhood!
Yet e'er in horror at my heinous crime
Thou turnest from me, hear me o my God:
T'is thou who plantest deep within our breast
The sacred love unto the land that bore us!
Thou giv'st to man his arm of powerful strength,
Unto his brain it's thoughts of prudent council,
That he should watch o'er and protect the land
That gave him birth and lent to him it's language,
That wondrous heritage of humankind!
Cast me for ever from thy holy presence,
Yet let the stroke that hurls me to the depths,
Bring desolation on the traitor's head!

Edward.

An oath upon the holy crucifix!
God's cherub standeth with a flaming sword
To guard o'er such an oath.

Harold.

      I know it well.

Edward.

Who breaks it is accurst.

Harold.

      I know it well.

Edward.

Such courage there can be? I had not thought it. —
Yet promise me that on the judgement day
Thou'lt say to the almighty: Edward warned me.

Harold.

That will I sire.

Edward.

     Call bishop Stigand hither.

Harold.

What is thy purpose?

Edward.

     Swift! The bishop Stigand!

(Harold opens the door R.)

Harold.

The king desires thy presence bishop Stigand!

*(Enter **Stigand** from R.).*

What is thy will?

Edward.

     Haste bishop — haste bring hither
Th' insignia of the heavy weighing honour,
Beneath the which I've sighed my life away,
.The royal crown!

128

Stigand.
Sire?

Edward.
Hasten — question not!
Let every bell in London's town be rung,
The nobles and the people call —

Stigand.
I hasten.
(exit C.)

Edward.
Heir of my crime, until the end shall come,
Our paths must be most closely interwoven.
To thee I leave the glittering, thorny crown
That decketh kings! T'is nothing good I give thee —

Harold.
To each and every word thou speakest sire
My heart gives solemn answer, „Yea and „Amen".

(Enter **Gytha, Morcar, Edwin** from L.).

Gytha.
Thou tell'st me things that sound so wondrous strange —
Thus to pass by me —

Morcar.
Yonder doth he stand,
See if thou knowest him.

Gytha (stands still).
My son, my Harold!

Harold (hastening toward her and embracing her).

O mother, mother, best of earthly treasures.

Gytha (tenderly).

Thy countenance shews traces of hard days,
That well may be for thou wast 'midst thy foes,
Cowards alone return unscathed from combat —
Thou gav'st me not the joy of thy first greeting —
Important duties led thee to the king?
Not so my son?

Harold.

So t'was beloved mother.

Gytha.

I knew it well — thou had'st no other reason —
Thy duty is fulfilled — remember now
How long I have been parted from my children.
Where is my youngest son, thy brother Wulfnoth?
(pause.)
Speak stony lips, say, say — where is my child?
(she starts back in terror).
O heavenly father shield me from distraction!

Harold.

Mother —

Gytha.

And yet it is my Harold's voice —
I can be patient — was my darling dead
When thou cam'st o'er the sea? Or did duke William
Refuse to give the child to thee again?
If me thou hear'st not, hear the voice of God. —

Harold.

O mother ask not now, ask not to-day.

130

Gytha.

Did she forlid it?

Harold.
She?

Gytha.

What is't thou wearest
Around thy neck? What gleamoth there so brightly?
I know it — t'is the visage of the viper
That stole away from me my Harold's soul!

(she stretches out her hand and attempts to seize the picture.)

Harold (grasping her arm).

And had'st thou given unto me ten lives
Instead of one — take hence thy hand — I charge thee!

Gytha
(raises her arm and thrusts back the sleeve of her robe).

Here is the spot — gaze one and all upon it —
Where with his cruel glove of steel he grasped me!
These were the arms that into life have born him;
The child's soft curly locks flowed brightly round them
This hand hath pointed out to him in youth,
The hills and valleys of his native land.
Yes, yes, these arms have been to him a cradle
O'erfilled with all things noble here on earth —
This is the day on which he spurned them from him,
To give himself unto a Norman wench.

Harold.

Almighty, hear her not — it is my mother
That slandereth thine angel! Let thy thunder
Fall on my head!

Gytha.

     Ah Harold had it fallen,
That day on which thou wentest to the Normans
(to Edwin and Morcar.)

I know ye're glad to see me fall so deeply!
Yes, I was proud of him — yet not too proud!
I loved him — ay I loved him and so well
That his foul treason makes my heart a desert!
Did ever mother weep such tears as these;
Too great the misery this heart must bear!

(The bells begin ringing. **Stigand** enters from the back of the stage carrying
the crown on a purple cushion: The curtains are drawn aside and a great crowd
of people is seen: Amongst them stand **Ordgar, Edric, Baldwulf**).

Stigand.

Called hither by the solemn pealing bell,
The people flock unto the palace gates,
Here at thy feet my sovereign I lay
This precious sign —

Edward.

     Hence — let me not behold it!
Plague of my days and torment of my nights,
The sign of curses pressed upon my brow!
My life's tree shaken by a deadly frost
Casts forth from it the hated parasite
That fed upon the marrow of it's peace.
Away, away — let madmen in their fury
Tear limb from limb for thy deceitful glitter —
Unto the wildest raver I bequeath thee!

Stigand.

T'is good — the royal crown is but of metal —
But unto whom dost thou bequeath thy people?

132

Harold.

They are bequeathed together with the crown.

Morcar and Edwin.

To whom?

Harold.

To me!

Morcar.

Hold hold, what meaneth this?

Stigand.

One word, king Edward, speak thou but one word:
Wilt thou that Harold at thy death be king?

Edward.

I make him heir unto my crowned torments.

Morcar.

This youth our king?

Edward.

Nay rather say this man
Who knoweth things the which alone to know
Can change the careless countenance of youth
Into the frozen visage of old age!

Morcar.

What knows he more than we do?

Edward.

Future things
Rising aloft in dark and bloody clouds
Of destiny —

133

Edwin.

Ah these are fever dreamings.

Edward.

No dreams are these! The shadowy hand of death
Openeth prophetically ear and eye;
I hear the rushing, whirring wheel of time
Shaken by storms, yet rolling ever on,
Crumbling and crushing towns and lands beneath it;
Between it's spokes wells forth the blood of nations,
The track it leaves — the race of humankind —
And he alone from out the human mass,
Who shaketh off the trammels of his conscience,
Purged from all weakness by hell's glowing flame,
He dares to seize the spokes and bid them stay;
Such one I know —
(gazing fixedly at Harold.)
Give unto him the crown.

Stigand *(to Harotd).*

Receive the crown then Harold from my hands,
And from my mouth receive the first allegiance.

Harold
(taking the crown from the cushion).

Come now thou circlet — fashioned golden serpent,
Glide round my head and with thine icy breath
Freeze up and kill remembrance in my brain
Of all that maketh beings mild and holy.
All feeling that exists within my breast
I forge into one iron stern resolve:
(he sets the crown upon his head.)
Here William, Norman Duke, behold the answer
That Harold, Saxon king to thee doth give!

Ordgar.

Hail to king Harold!

People (shouting)

Hail to Godwin's son!

Harold (to Edwin and Morcar).

Ye heard the words your master, Edward spoke,
Do me allegiance.

Morcar.

Good, we both are ready
To swear obedience with our hearts and hands
When first thy mother shall have done thee homage.

Harold (in a low voice to his mother).

Dost thou not mark the serpent's cloven tongue
Of evil malice hidden 'neath these words?
Destroy the hopes they cherish o my mother,
Speak that which they are loth from thee to hear.

Gytha (speaking low, her gaze averted).

First tell me what thou did'st in Normandy.

Harold.

I'll tell thee breast to breast and eye to eye,
But ask it not in presence of the people,
For England's weal. —

Gytha.

O speak not of thy country,
For I have gathered from thy gloomy words
Thou hast betrayed it.

Edward.
> Homage, Countess!

Gytha (after an inword conflict).
> Never!
(she turns quickly away and goes out.)

Harold.

Mother!

Morcar (to Edwin).

I stay no longer, goest thou with me?

Edwin.

I go with thee; We will to horse!

Edward.
> Remain!

With the last breath of this my dying breast,
With the last gasp of this my fleeting life,
I bid ye do him homage!

Morcar.
> Let him fetch it

From out my castle!

Harold.
> I shall come!

Morcar.
> Ay come thou,

But bring thou scaling ladders and good weapons,
For my high walls like granite lips shall hold
These words „I do refuse thee my allegiance."
(Morcar and Edwin exeunt R.)

—◄ ACT 4. ►—

Edward (rising with difficulty).

Ye shall not hence (falls back) God help me — icy death
Creeps up into my breast —

Stigand

See, see the king
He groweth pale!

Edward.

Lift up my chair — I bid ye —
And bear me forth from this accursed life.

(the chair is lifted up.)

Let me but die in peace — woe woe is me,
And woe to the lost people of the Saxons!

(he is carried out.)

Ordgar

(approaches Harold, the people comes into the hall).

I neither know nor do I understand
What here was spoken, — this alone I know,
That when the gallows were stretched out to seize me,
That when all hope of life had died away
In death's last terror — sudden o'er my head
There floated like a cherub's outspread wings
Thy noble charger's snowy, flowing mane —
Know how that moment bending from thy saddle
Thou struck'st the hangman with a deadly blow
Down to the ground — Harold my well loved lord,
May God Almighty's thunder smite me down,
Had I another single word than this;
God bless our Harold, England's lawful king!

(he kneels before him and kisses his hand.)

The People (pressing round him).
Harold, the son of Godwin, shall be king!

Edric (seizing his hand).
Hail to king Harold!

Baldwulf.
Hail to Harold, hail!

Harold (raising his hands to heaven).
So hear me Thou whose bright and lofty throne
The stars like flaming satellites surround;
Hear me now pledge unto the Saxon people
Each thought, each feeling of my heart and soul:
My body be it's shield, my arm it's weapon!
It's foe my foe, it's grave my grave!

Stigand.
God hears it.

Ordgar.
We swear our true obedience to king Harold,
So long our arm hath power to wield the axe!

People.
We swear that we'll be true to him!

Stigand.
God hears it.

Transformation.

Scene 2.

(A vestibule in London palace. Doors R. and L. The street is seen between columns at the back of the stage. L. a raised throne. Over the throne a waving banner surrounded with axes. Night, torches are attached to the walls).

Several royal Attendants.

(The first Attendant stands gazing at the heavens, then turns to the others.)

First Attendant.

Come hither, see from here t'is clear to view.

(the others approach.)

There — where my finger points to —

Second Attendant.

            See, ah see!
A grewsome thing — as t'were a rod of fire
It stretcheth o'er the heavens from north to south.
Is it a star?

First Attendant.

          A comet t'is they call it;
I'ne heard it said that in a hundred years
It comes but once, but when it doth appear
It evil times portendeth.

Second Attendant.

          That may be —
Ne'er saw I such a thing.

First Attendant.

        Hark, hark what noise?

(A great crowd of men women and children appear outside the columns from L.
In their midst is a fantastically dressed old man carrying a harp — the people
remain standing at the entrance to the hall).

The old Man (with loud voice).

The heavens burn, the time is now fulfilled!
The hour of dread our fathers prophesied,
The last dread hour is come!

(Enter **Edric. Baldwulf** (from the street).

Edric (to the people).

Go homeward, go!
(to the old man.)

Why terrify the people?

People.

Let him speak!

The old Man.

List to the prophesy our fathers made us:
When first a king shall come who breaketh oaths,
When from the southern shore the wind shall blow,
And the chastizing star flames red in heaven,
Then shall the Norman ride upon the waves;
Evil times will come, times of dread and evil,
Then shall the Saxon people cease to be.

Edric.

But who then is the king that breaketh oaths?

Baldwulf.

Tear out his tongue, the bird of evil omen!

(Enter **Ordgar** from R. to the former).

Say, have ye seen this strange, this grewsome thing?

Edric.

Be silent!

Ordgar.
Have ye seen the wondrous star?

Edric.

Art thou infected with the people's terror?

Ordgar.
Who I? I fear? — And yet the times are evil.
Come on ye furious howling Norman wolves
For like the angry bull I've horns and hoofs
To trample ye to death e'er ye destroy me:

A Woman (shrieking).
Normans are in the land!

Edric.
It is not true!

A Woman.
Why does the king forsake us?

People.
Ay! — the king!
the people press into the hall, the Attendants try to force them back.)

First Attendant (raising his hellebard).
Back — back — ye dare not enter —

Edric.

See good sirs,
We are but as the cork upon the waters,
. The billows hear us on.

(the people, carrying Edric, Baldwulf and Ordgar forward with them, press into the hall.)

People.

The king? the king?

Edric.

They know not what they do for very terror!

(Enter a **Herald** from L. blowing a trumpet).

Place for the king, king Harold son of Godwin!

(Enter **Harold** ffrom L. (armed).

Ordgar.

Hail to the king, the people's safeguard!

People.

Hail!

Harold (ascending the steps of the throne).
Why come ye thronging to your monarch's throne
In such wild tumult, at the sacred hour
When nature sends her messenger of peace,
Sleep that makes enemy and friend as one,
Changeth our troubled thoughts to quiet rest,
And raging passion into childlike dreams?

(the Women throw themselves at the foot of the throne.)

Women.

Save us king Harold!

People.

Harold — save us — save us!

Harold.

Have I then so forgot a monarch's duty,
That ye must raise such piercing cry of terror
To mind me of it?

A Woman.

See the heavens threaten!
Normans are in the land!

Harold.

Who is't that says so?

(a voice at the back of the stage.)

Make place, make place for worthy Bishop Stigand.

*(Enter **Stigand, Wilfried** from the back)*

Stigand.

My lord and master, from the Norman's land
This priest as messenger to thee hath come.

Ordgar.

From Normandy?

Edric.

What message doth he bring?

(all press round the throne following Stigand and Wilfried.)

Stigand.

He left for England many weeks ago,
But adverse winds detained him, as he tells me
Till now.

Harold.

Why cometh he to me at night?
Is this a fitting time to bring a message?

Wilfried

(who has till now stood with his eyes cast to the ground raises his head suddenly

T'was charged me that so soon my foot should touch
The soil of England were it day or night,
I should announce to thee what now thou'lt hear.

Harold (gazing at Wilfried).

Where have I seen this countenance? — Thou comest
From o'er the sea, from Normandy?

Wilfried.

It is so.
(a murmur arises amongst the people).

Harold.

The Duke of Normandy hath sent thee hither?

Wilfried.

Not so king Harold.

Harold.
No?

Wilfried.

Another sends me.
It is —

Harold.

Hold -- hold — I know from whence thou comest. (in low tones).
T'is from the church?

Wilfried (loud and distinctly).

It is the church that sends me.

Harold (whispering to him.)

At peril of thy life — be still, be still! (aloud.)
Ye all have heard: He comes not from the Norman,
The message that from holy church he bringeth,
Is for mine ear alone — ye all can go!

Wilfried (pressing his hands upon his heart.)
(aside.)

It is thy will inexorable God. (aloud to Harold.)
The church's word is not for thee alone.

Harold.

Peace if thy life thou lovest!

Wilfried.

Sire, my life
I love not, and I dare not hold my peace. — (raising his voice.)
Thus speaketh he to whom God gave the power
To bind and to make loose, to open widely
The gates of paradise or aye to close them:
Because thou'st broken thy most sacred oath —

Stigand.

Thy oath?

Wilfried.

Upon the holy crucifix,
That William duke of Normandy should be
The king of England after Edward's death. —

Harold (striking his forehead.)

O endless night! Let now thy jaws engulph me.

People.

Betrayed! Betrayed!

Ordgar.

Ah woe! And it is true?
O tell us that such oath thou n'er hast sworn!

Wilfried (elevating his voice.)

For this thou ne'er shalt dwell where dwell the blest,
But amidst gnashing teeth and grewsome wailings,
And never shalt thou taste the joys of heaven;
Be thou accurst in life — in death — for ever!
Curst be the soil on which thy foot doth tread:
Curst all who follow thee in true obedience,
And all who love thee be like thee — accurst! —

(aside.)

T'is o'er — have mercy on my soul o God!

(a long gloomy silence.)

(The people crowd together in whispering groups — first singly, then in masses
the people rush towards the doors at the back of the stage leaving Harold, Stigand
Ordgar, Wilfried and the Attendants in the hall.)

Harold.

Close up the palace gates! Ye Saxons, hear me!

(The Attendants rush to the doors und force the crowd back into the hall.)

Ordgar.

Stay! listen to the king! Speak gracious Sire!

Edric.

The oath thou'st taken?

Harold.

Mighty God of heaven,
Hast thou thy stars to light the skies alone?
O shet their light upon this black deceit!

Edric.

The oath -- thou'st sworn?

Harold.

An oath — yet ⋯ yet not this!

A Woman.

He swore! — Ye hear it!

Edric.

And with him we're curst!

Baldwulf.

We'll not to hell with him! make place!

People.

Make place!

(The people rush upon the Attendants who endeavour to defend the doors but are
pushed aside, a part of the crowd flies from the hall in wild tumult.)

Ordgar (throwing himself upon the ground.

Deep be the grave in which Earl Godwin sleeps
That of his son's vile deed he nothing hear!

Harold.

Break not o heart; burst not o seething brain!

(to Wilfried.)

Ha! thou accursed bringer of damnation,
Thou art a Saxon?

Wilfried.

Yea — and serve my God.

Harold

What ho attendants!

(to Wilfried.)

To thy God I'll send thee,
Tell Him thou comest from thy country's king
Who struck thee down as had'st thou been a viper!

(two attendants advance right and left of Wilfried with drawn swords.)

Stigand.

Harold — have mercy on him, spare him, spare him!

Harold.

Away! strike! strike!

(the attendants strike him to the ground.)

Wilfried (sinking supported by Stigand.)

Have mercy on me — Jesus —
O bishop Stigand — holy priest of God,
Child of the Saxon people as am I,
And therefore dear unto my very soul;
Now at this hour when death draws grimly near me
To end a life deceived and most unblest,
Let me impart to thee a fearful secret
That weigheth heavily upon my soul.

Stigand.

Tell me what troubleth thee?

Wilfried.
The grewsome oath —

Stigand.
What meanest thou?

Wilfried.
It was a traiterous oath
Contrived and plotted with a hellish cunning
By bishop Robert and the Norman William,
Duke Harold to betray.

Stigand.
Whom? Harold?

Wilfried.
Harold!
Myself was present on that day at Rouen
When they together planned to forge that oath —
Lift up my head — my tongue is growing heavy —
Ah death befree me — it was crime and treason
For Harold knew not what it was he swore!

Stigand.
Why wert thou silent then before the people?

Wilfried.
Archbishop Robert charged me to keep silence.

Stigand.
A curse upon him!

Wilfried.
Father — did I wrong?

Stigand.

Lost one — most wrong.

Wilfried.

O Robert of Jumièges
Give back to me once more my cheated life:
Dread death — release me, free me from thy grasp —
This heart that n'eer was foe to human creature
Trod down like poisonous worm —

Harold (bending overhim).

Unhappy priest,
Thy blood weighs heavily upon my soul.

Wilfried.

My king — my king — my well beloved — master —
(dies.)

(Enter **the Abbot and 12 Monks of Hyde monastery** — they wear
black cowls and advance to the front of the stage singing:)

Dies irae, dies illa
Solvet saecla in favilla.

Harold.

What bring to me these birds of evil omen?
What bring ye?

Abbot.

What our garments tell thee: war!

(the Abbot and the 12 Monks thow off their cowls shewing that they are clad
in armour.)

Abbot.

Arise king Harold, up ye Saxon people!
The tiger swam across the ocean waves,
The Normans are in England.

Harold.

Death and hell!

Abbot.

We from our cloister, that on stony cliff
Looks southward far and wide across the sea,
Beheld them nearing in seven hundred ships,
And at the moment when their fearful Duke
In wildest rage of fieverish impatience
Leapt with a bound upon the English shore,
Their war-cry overwhelmed the thundering flood —

Harold.

Where stand the Normans?

Abbot.

Near to hastings.

Harold.

Good,
Now in the history of the fate of worlds,
The name of Hastings shall by those names stand
That in the book are writ with crimson letters;
Fate on these names hath laid it's blood-stained hand,
To point them out to future generations
Reminding them — „on such a day it happened."

Stigand.

Thou speak'st of dying e'er thou go'st to battle;
Gaze but around thee — thou art left alone!

Harold (spreading out his arms).

I have two lions still to do me service,
Upon the Norman William they shall spring
And do him murder 'midst his very host!
Give me mine axe and saddle quick my charger.

(he tears the banner from the wall and flings it into the midst of the hall.)

Here cast I down the banner of the Saxon,
Who dares to lift it up?

Ordgar (seizes the banner).

To me the banner!

Harold.

Yes! Thou, thou weird memento of my country,
Shalt fight to-day beside me!

Ordgar.

Son of Godwin,
These hands inseverable from this banner,
This life with iron chains enchained to thine,
In life, in death, where thou art — I will be!

Stigand.

Entrench thyself behind the walls of London,
List to my warning, go not forth to battle!

Harold.

Speak not to me of caution at this hour,
The one, sole law that it obeys is vengeance!
Come fate, draw near, waft tempest and destruction,
Shipper and ship o'erwhelm in one great wreck
Thou dost affright but those who fear the end!
The present moment giveth me the law,
And it's fulfilment: combat until death!
It is your king that calls — who'll follow?

All.

All!

Harold
(seizes an axe from an attendant and waves it aloft.)

And must we perish, ocean o'er our grave
Shall sing our death-song with her thundering voice,
And rolling on for centuries untold,
Shall bear from land to land the lofty tidings,
The Anglosaxon people great and glorious,
Went forth, their king before them, unto death!
(rushes out.)

Ordgar.
Their king before them! Hail!

All.
Hail, Harold hail!
(all follow Harold wildly out.)

The Curtain falls.

End of the 4th Act.

Act 5.

Scene 1.

(A low gloomy vault; doors L. — in the middle a portal secured by closed iron gates in front of it.)

Seneschal. Eleanor.

Seneschal.

I pray thee let not the princess come hither;
Tell her, as is the truth, the Duke forliddeth
Most rigidly, admittance to the child.

Eleanor.

All this I told her, but I spoke in vain,
She heeds me not, and comes to see the child.

Seneschal.

It is a piteous, lamentable sight.

(Enter **Adéle**, **Alice** from L. to the former.

Adéle.

Unkind one, why would'st thou prevent my coming?
Are ye then one and all forsworn against me?

154

Alice.

Ah look upon me; know'st thou me no more
My sweet princess? — see, see it is thine Alice.
T'is not unkind that I do so beseech thee
To come and leave this drear and gloomy spot.

Adéle.

A haunt of terror — ay — a fitting dwelling
For a forsaken child.
(to the Seneschal.)
                    Thou art the man,
Who doth withhold my child from me? — restore him!

Seneschal.

Princess it was thy father who forbade me —

Adéle.

I have a greater right unto this child
Than hath my father — give the child to me.
See there, behind that door — t'is there he lies?
For pity's sake — I pray thee — pray thee — open —
(she falls down before the door weeping.)

Seneschal.

As warder was this post to me entrusted,
But not as hangman — come, make place, so be it!
(he unfastens the bolts of the door and opens it.)

(**Wulfnoth** is seen lying on a low bed.)

Adéle.

Still still, be silent — wake him not, he sleeps. —
At other times, in sleep his downy cheeks

Were red as roses — now they are so pale. —
White — white as snow — how motionless he lies —
(she grasps Alice by the hand.)
Mine eyes deceive me — is it not so Alice?
Else — I could almost think — dost feel his breath?
Speak — speak! Thou feelest it?

Seneschal.

     Hence, hence away,
Princess, I do beseech of thee —

Adéle.

       This child —
Alice, methinks — this child — this child - is dead!!
Wulfnoth!
(casts herself upon the bed.)

Seneschal.

   O this is worse than I had thought it.
(pause.)

Adéle
(rises, gazing as if unconsciously around her.)
Which of ye was it said? —

Alice.

     That said — dear mistress?
What did'st thou hear?

Adéle.

Methought they said that Harold —
Harold were dead.

Eleanor.

    No, no, we never said so.

156

Adéle.

Harold is dead. —

(she advances slowly toward the front of the stage gazing into vacancy.)

Ah see — see there — see there ...

Alice.

What seest thou?

Adéle.

     I see a vast   vast field,
Strewn with the dead — and there — there in their midst —
See — there — see, see, ah woe! ah woe! who did it?

Alice.

Did what? Great heaven, did what?

Seneschal.

     This troubled spirit
Doth hold a direful wandering in the future.

Adéle.

Ah — how disfigured are his well loved features —
Into his very eye they shot the arrow,
The cruel arrow, why then into that
I loved so well — o husband — o beloved —

(She knee's down on the ground, with a motion as if bending over some one dying before her.)

Eleanor.

She must from hence.

(Eleanor and Alice raise her from the ground.)

Adéle.

     Ah do not tear me from him.
Let me rest by him! See ye not yon rider

Approach in wild career — ah hold — ah hold —
Hold up thy steed — thou crushest him — o God! —
Open thy vizier that I see thy face!
Jesus have mercy on me, t'is my father!
To rest beloved one, go thou to rest,
Adéle comes to rock thee into sleep —
I come — I come! —

(her maidens lead her away.)

Transformation.

Scene 2.

The battle field of hastings. night. a hilly landscape the sea is seen at the back of
the stage. L. and R. — high, rocky cliffs — from the cliff R. — a path leads
from the rocks to the front of the stage. At the foot of the cliff L. the ground is
somewhat deeper.)

(Enter **Gytha, Stigand, and the Abbot of Hyde** from L. their faces
concealed in large black cloaks. The Abbot and Stigand carry forches.)

Abbot.

Black is the night as is the fate of England —
Bring here thy torch that we may further seek him.

Stigand.

I fear, I fear our search will be in vain.
An arrow pierced his eye.

Abbot.

Yes, so it chanced.
The arrow entered to the very shaft —
He tore it forth and broke it into fragments
Then wildly fought again.

158

Stigand.

And as he fell,
The Norman horses trampled o'er his body.

Abbot.

Had they but sent to us some troops from London
The day were ours; full three times did he turn
His head, the blood all streaming down, toward London —
None came!

Gytha.

No, no, they all forsook their king
In hour of deadly need — they will repent it.

Abbot (pointing upwards).

Here it must be — alone, upon this rock,
Close to the edge, the king stood in the fight —
From thence I saw his gold-locked head sink down.

Stigand to the countess).

If thou hast strength to bear it, Countess, come!
(Stigand and the abbot commence ascending the path that leads to the cliff — Gytha
stops suddenly at a spot where the ground becomes somewhat deeper, she bends down
then presses her hands upon her heart and remains for a moment motionles).

Gytha.

In death — how like he is unto his father!

Abbot
(turning back and speaking in low tones to Stigand).

See — what was that —

Stigand.

Her son is found?

Abbot.

T' would seem so.

(Stigand and the Abbot retrace their steps to where Gytha is standing, and let the
light of their torches fall on the spot where the body of Harold is lying.)

Gytha (kneels down beside the body).

I pained thee son, because thou gav'st me pain —
Ah woe, that at the last it should have been so —
Pride of my soul — my son — my noble son —

Stigand (weeping).

Accept these tears, the last thy people shed,
As only tribute, o beloved King
They in their miséry to thee can offer.

(Enter **William, Odo, Randolf, Montgomery** coming down the path
from cliff R. Some Attendants carry torches.)

Abbot.

I hear the sound of voices — torches near us —
Help me to bear the body hence
    (The Abbot and Stigand prepare to carry the dead Harold away).

William (bending forward over the rock).

Remain!
Whose body is it that ye bury there?

Abbot.

The Lord have mercy — t'is the Norman Duke.
        (they retire from the body.)

William.

Whom have ye?

160

ACT 5.

Gytha (rises and advances to the front).

See thyself if thou can'st dare it.

William.

Who speaks? A woman?

Odo,
With a woman's boldness.

Myself will see —

(Odo and Randulf go quickly down the path — Odo tears back the covering from Gytha's head.)

Gytha.
Dost know now who I am?

Odo.

Earl Godwin's wife!

Gytha.
And mother of his sons!

William
(who has descended the path with Montgomery in the meanwhile).

I would behold this dead man's countenance —
Bring torches hither!

Randulf lighting up the body of Harold).
Gracious Duke, t'is Harold!

William.

Harold is mine! Upon the ocean shore
Where t'is most waste and drear, there make his grave;
I would be a sin to give him christian burial:
Hence, Countess Gytha — hence — away, away —
Thy Harold resteth here.

Gytha.

I do implore thee,
Give me my son and I from hence will go
Without a word — nought, nought to thee I'll say
Of all that well I might —

Odo.

Nay hear this woman!
The Duke perchance should fear her?

Gytha.

Thou may'st mock!
Thy master knows what I would say.

William.

By God,
Go not too far — I tell thee that the perjured —

Gytha.

Wake not the wrath of God with sinful oath!
An hour will come more terrible than this,
When neither host nor victory can help thee,
Nor yet the comfort that thy fraud invented!
Before thee God will then unveil his face,
Threatening and fearful as this fearful night,
And in one balance will ye then be weighed,
Robert and thou 'gainst Harold, 'gainst my son —

Randolf.

Peace frenzied prophetess —

Gytha.

Ye two together,
Will weigh the lighter! Robert and Duke William,

Disturbers and destroyers of my house
Who even dare before death's solemn presence
To lie —

Odo.
Beware thou of Duke William's anger!

Gytha.
Fool that thou art, thou hast not stood as I have
By two lost sons: before me he must tremble,
If God he fears!

William.
      One single raving woman
Dares more than twenty men dare! hence! begone!

Gytha.
I swear I'll go not till my son thou giv'st me!

William.
If God doth give me not a special token,
I swear I will not give to thee thy son!

(Enter **The Seneschal** (coming down the path R.).

William.
What bring'st thou Seneschal with gloomy mien?

Seneschal.
With gloomy mien most gloomy tidings, Duke.

William.
Whence bringest thou such tidings?

Seneschal.

Duke, from Rouen;
Princess Adéle — thy sweet child — is dead.

William (covers his eyes with his hand).

Dead! — — — and when dying thought she of her father?

Seneschal.

One name alone dwelt on her pallid lips
With thousand pangs a thousand times repeated —

William.

That name? — —

Seneshal.

My Duke —

William.

The name?

Seneschal.

Was — Harold!

William.

Harold! — —
(pointing to Gytha.)

Give unto her the body of her son.

The Curtain falls.

The End.

The first Scene of the fifth Act

as given

in the royal Theatre

of

Berlin.

Act 5.

Scene 1.

(Adéles room in the palace at Rouen. A low vaulted chamber; a door L. In the background a window, before the window a couch: it is night, the chamber is faintly lighted).

(Adéle is seen lying upon the couch. Alice is seated beside her, Adéle's head resting upon her shoulder. Eleanor and the Seneschal stand together in the foreground.)

The Seneschal softly te Eleanor)
The lamp so faintly sheds it's scanty light
That scarce I should have known her: is't Adéle.
That resteth on yon couch?

Eleanor.
        Ay, ay, t'is she.
Ah see how grief hath paled her gentle visage.
Shew pity on her, grant her what she asks thee.

Seneschal.
O thou art cruel, to compel my duty
To hold such conflict with my pitying breast,
But yet the iron orders of the Duke
Lie like a bolt across the dungeon door
That closes on the child.

167

Eleanor.

Ah bring him hither —
The Duke will thank thee for thy disobedience
If it doth save his daughter; bring the child;
She's sleeping still — go.

Adéle (without changing her position).

Eleanor, thou errest,
I heeded every word that thou hast spoken
To this hard man.

Seneschal (approaching Adéle).

O do not call me hard,
My sweet, my gracious and most honoured mistress.

Adéle.

Kind sir — I've heard it said — God gave thee children?

Seneschal.

T'is true dear mistress.

Adéle.

Are those children young?
Thou lovest them?

Seneschal.

I pray to God each day
That he will guard my children.

Adéle.

Are my prayer
To thine I will unite. — O think good sir,
Think of an innocent, unhappy child

Soft as the gentle breath of early spring
That kisses tenderly the wintry earth,
A child incapable of doing hurt
And yet most capable of feeling grief —
And ah what sorrow! parted from it's mother;
Soothed by no murmurings of tender love;
A child that knoweth not that men can hate,
Punished for sins that it hath ne'er committed,
Enclosed within the gloomy night of prison.

Seneschal.

Enough, enough princess: each word thou speakest
So deeply moves me —

Adèle.

     In the wide, wide world
One heart alone that feels for this poor child
And yet unto this heart, thou wilt not give it?

Seneschal.

By God not I refuse it — but I pray thee
Ask not to see it, for this tender child;
Like flower transplanted from its native soil
Within the prison walls has drooped and faded.

Adéle (springs up).

I knew the child was ailing — let me go,
I'll to my child!

Alice.

    O mistress, dearest mistress
Be still, I pray thee hear me!

Adéle.

Stay me not!
Since thirty nights all sleep hath fled mine eyes
Because I heard the wailing of the child!
His countenance, once full of happy mirth,
Looks sorrowfully on me, and his hands
He stretches toward me — give me back my sleep.
Hard-hearted man, have I no power to move thee?

(she springs from her couch and casts herself at the feet of the Seneschal.)

Duke William's daughter lieth at thy feet,
Will thou not bring the child to me?

Seneschal.

Arise.
May God forbid that in the dust before me
Thou so should'st lie; whatever now may chance,
Be patient — I will bring to thee the child.

(exit hastily — L.)

Alice *(trying to raise Adéle).*

Come dearest, he will bring to thee thy darling,
This is no place for thee — come now and rest.

Adéle *(slowly rising).*

My limbs refuse to bear me — on my breast
There lies a heavy weight — I pray thee Alice
Open the casement — let me breathe the air.

(she reclines upon the couch.)

Alice.

The casement looketh north, the air is cold
And autumnlike — I bey thee swetest mistress
Let me refuse thee.

Adéle.

Eleanor come hither,
Thou hear'st she disobeys me —

Eleanor.

E'en as I,
For at this hour of night t'would be thy death.

Adéle.

If ye then both have so forsworn against me,
I will myself —

(Alice and Eleanor strive to hold her back.)

Be still — this air will kill me.

(she rises from her couch, throws open the winclow and leans out.)

Ah see — see there.

(pointing to the sky.)

Alice.

What seest thou Princess?

Adéle.

See yonder in the dark and gloomy heavens
That star that burneth like a blood-red torch.

(Alice and Eleanor advance to the window and gase out.)

Alice.

Ah! as thou say'st — it is an awful sight —
T'is like a sword that has been dipped in blood.

Eleanor.

T'is in the north.

Adéle.

The north — where England lieth.

(she advances to the front.)

Do ye not see — my father sailed northwards
With all his host — and he went forth to slay.
O'er Harold's head — that bloody star doth shine,
T'is the last greeting that my bridegroom sends me.

(she sinks in the arms of her ladies.)

Alice.

Ah no, not so dear lady —

Enter the **Seneschal** from L. to the former. He carries Wulfnoth in his arms — at the door he remains standing a moment).

Alice.

See who cometh:
The Seneschal doth bring to thee the child.

Adéle (raises her head).

Still, still, be silent, wake him not, he sleeps —
When first he came to me, his downy cheecks
Were red as roses — but to-day they're pale,
White, as the riven snow —

(she advances to him.)

My tender darling
Art thou so weary?

(she takes him in her arms.)

O — how cold and stiff
These little hands — come, close to me my child
And I will warm thee on mine own warm breast.

(she seats herself upon the couch taking the child on her knees.)

My sweet one — dost thou no more know Adéle?

(the child faintly opens his eyes and gazes at her bending his head with
a soft smile.)

Ah see this glance so full of bitter sorrow,
See this wan smile, the last pale fading reflex
Of the once happy blessedness of childhood.

(the arms of the child fall down at it's sides — it sinks back.)

Why dost thou take thine arms from off my neck?
Why do thine eyelids close? O Alice! — Alice! —
Come here and place thy hand upon his heart —
Dost feel it's beating?

Alice

(softly touches Wulfnoth, then falls upon her knees and covers her face with
her hands).

           By th' Almighty God,
Princess — I almost think — this child — is —

Adéle.
Dead?!

(she bends over the child, presses it to her heart, covers it with kisses, then lets her
head sink upon it's breast.)

(pause.)

Adéle (again raising her head).

List to my words! Unstained and innocent,
This soul returneth to the arms of God,
From whence it came; it's God will know it well,
For all unchanged it's image will return. —
A countenance I know that this one likeneth;
A soul I know, that to this soul resembles:
Pure as is this one, true and free from guile.
By all the world deceived and betrayed,
By one alone well known and well beloved,

Thy soul t'is, Harold — thine, my faithful bridegroom!

(she rises spectrelike from the couch, the child in her arms.)

My father gave this child into my hands
And said t'was Harold's heart — I hold it Harold,
Close to mine own and to my lips I press it,
And with this pledge of love within mine arms
I tread the long dark journey unto thee —
Open thine arms — my Harold — ope them wide —
We come — my Harold — unto thee — we come —

(she falls back lifeless on her couch.)

The Curtain falls.

Errata.

www.ingramcontent.com/pod-product-compliance
Lightning Source LLC
Chambersburg PA
CBHW030613040726
47497CB00008B/2960